COMPLICATION

Chronicles of the Uprising: 2

K.A. Salidas

Complication
ISBN 978-0-9851277-7-0
Copyright © 2014 by K.A. Salidas

Cover Layout by Willsin Rowe http://willsinrowe.blogspot.com/
Interior Layout by Katie Salidas http://www.katiesalidas.com
Editing by Sharazade http://sharazade.com/?p=825

Published by:
Rising Sign Books
http://www.risingsignbooks.net

For more information about my books email:
katiesalidas@gmail.com

CHRONICLES OF THE UPRISING

Dissension - The great cataclysm wiped almost all life from the face of planet Earth, but tiny pockets of survivors crawled from the ashes, with only one thought: survival, at any cost.

But not all survivors were human.

In the dark, militant society that has risen in the aftermath, vampires, once thought to be mythical, have been assimilated and enslaved. Used for blood sport their lives are allowed to continue only for the entertainment of the masses. Reviled as savages, they are destined to serve out their immortal lives in the arena, as gladiators.

And there is no greater gladiator than Mira: undefeated, uncompromising...and seemingly unbreakable. When an escape attempt leads Mira into the path of Lucian Stavros, the city's Regent, her destiny is changed forever.

Lucian, raised in a culture which both reviles and celebrates the savagery and inhumanity of vampires, finds Mira as intriguing as she is brash. An impulsive decision - to become Mira's patron – changes more than just Lucian's perception about vampire kind. The course of his life is altered in ways he could never have predicted – a life that is suddenly as expendable as hers.

Can Mira prove to Lucian that all is not as it seems? Can Lucian escape centuries of lies, bloodshed, and propaganda to see the truth? Or will the supreme power of the human overlords destroy them both?

Complication - Narrowly escaping death at the hands of the Magistrate, Mira travels west, toward the coast. With three weakened human fugitives accompanying her, she searches for the mythical land of Sanctuary.

After encountering a pack of wolf shifters, headed by the charismatic—and brazen—Stryker, Mira learns that Sanctuary is real after all. Caldera Grove: home of the Otherkin. Hidden in the mouth of a dormant volcano, it has protected its residents from humans since the early days following the great cataclysm. For Mira— a vampire— Caldera Grove is a land of peace; an escape from the relentless persecution of the humans who once enslaved her, and an end to the daily struggle and bloodshed of being a gladiator.

For the humans accompanying her, Caldera Grove means death. Humans, greedy and untrustworthy creatures, are destroyed before they can penetrate its borders.

To plead her case for entry into Caldera, Mira must abandon her companions, albeit temporarily, and follow Stryker into the heart of the city. What she finds within Caldera Grove presents her with an unenviable decision between her own desires for freedom and peace, or honor and the human companions who risked it all for her.

Revolution - Peace is an illusion. Blood, violence, and death follow Mira like shadows.

Battle lines have been drawn between human and Otherkin, and a bloody war is on the horizon: one that will end in either a shift in the world's balance of power...or ultimate destruction.

In spite of their strength, powers, and a rage known only by the oppressed, the Otherkin are evenly matched by the superior numbers of the human army. To tip the balance in their favor, the Otherkin need more soldiers – and their only options are the Gladiators of New Haven city.

Mira is sent across enemy lines to recruit any able-bodied vampires to her cause. But what she discovers along the way will blur the lines between friends and enemies. Seeds of doubt weaken Mira's allegiance, and she finds herself torn between the old masters who used her as entertainment and the new ones who consider her as nothing more than a weapon.

As the war draws near, Mira will have to decide what she is truly fighting for.

Transition - Peace is just a breath between battles for Mira. Hardened by slavery and war, she longs for the simpler life, knowing that it might never be hers to enjoy. There is always another battle waiting to be fought, another foe on the horizon. Peace between humans, vampires, and otherkin may be nothing more than a dream, but Mira holds out hope. It is during this brief respite that Mira is gifted one of her greatest weapons. Though it brings with it memories of a time when she was not so jaded, it also comes with a reminder of terrible pain and loss. Awakening deeply hidden emotions within her, if Mira can use this to her advantage, she'll have a new ally in the next battle to come.

**More Titles planned. For more information visit
www.KatieSalidas.com**

CHAPTER ONE

T housands of twinkling stars lit the night sky above, a glorious sight Mira had not seen in more years than she could count. Their majesty stole the breath from her chest. Night called her like a siren's song both familiar and strange. Imprisoned deep under the ground as she'd been all those long years, not even allowed to smell the crispness of night air, the melody had long since been forgotten but never truly lost. More than a delicacy, it called forth primal urges, reaching some long-repressed savage part of her. It was all Mira could do not to pull the vehicle over and take off into the wild, but the trio of humans riding along with her, escaping to safety, needed her to remain on task.

Eyes riveted to the rugged landscape behind them, Mira screened the horizon for any signs of pursuit. The badlands—a mix of ruined forest and parched hard-packed dirt—stretched out as far as the eye could see. Regular monsoon flooding had made the land tough and treacherous. Their transport, not equipped for off-roading, jolted and rocked, banged and bumped as it sped on between gnarled trees and mountainous boulders.

Hours had passed since their daring escape from New Haven city behind the Iron Gate walls, one of the eight human city-states and the westernmost point of the Northern continent.

Though there had been no sign of their vehicle being followed, Mira was not yet ready to stop for a break. She had no clue of the capability and reach of the humans beyond their city walls. The last thing she wanted was to give in to fatigue too soon and end up right back where she started… in prison.

Painful memories drove her to her task. Thirty long years she'd been enslaved; thirty years of torture, pain, violence, and bloodshed… all of it under the orders of her human masters. Olivia's face flashed through her mind. Her former owner. If she'd only had the opportunity to pay the pampered princess back for the vile things she'd had endured. The things she'd been forced to do. Countless vampires she'd been forced to kill. Cold dead eyes of numerous victims haunted her dreams, and probably would for the rest of her immortal life.

Killing had been her way of life. Survival. Kill or be killed. As a gladiator, there was no middle ground. In the arena, by order of her masters, she'd sent so many others to early graves. It was enough to make her hungry for revenge on all members of the so-called human race. The lot of them were untrustworthy, greedy, vengeful, lying bastards.

Mira shot a heated glance toward Lucian. Human. Former Regent. One who had, in the past, ordered the death of many of her kind. At a single turn of his thumb she herself had been forced to end the lives of many vampire kin, ripping out their throats while crowds cheered above her.

And they called *her* a savage. Mira scoffed at the irony.

She should hate Lucian as much as she hated the rest of human society; she certainly had the right to. But not all humans were bad. At least not that one, she reminded herself as her gaze narrowed down his short dark hair toward the crook of his neck, spotting the pulsating artery there. It would be so easy to sink her fangs in and drink her fill. Lucian had once been part of the problem, but no longer. He'd helped save her from her imprisonment. He'd proven his true nature. She looked back to the other two humans in the vehicle – the aging Curtis and his wife, Sarah, huddling together, fighting exhaustion. They too had helped, despite obvious revulsion at her species. Not all humans were the enemy. Not all were evil. Just as she, a vampire, was not evil.

She dragged in another breath of that glorious fresh night air and let it clear away the anger. So many years she had dreamed of freedom, and now she had it.

She was free. Alive. No more silver shackles. No more tiny cell smelling of dirt and decay. No more fighting for her life in the arena. Sure, they were still in danger, and the humans would certainly pursue her, but in this one moment, she was free. The crispness of that single breath stirred within her the desire for more. Others too should savor this freedom. She thought back to the prison and all of the vampires still trapped within. George, the closest thing she'd had to a true friend. Tegan, her last opponent. He'd been her enemy in the arena and in training, but he didn't deserve to remain locked behind silver-coated bars. Countless others were still languishing away within the Iron Gate prison. Those poor souls. They needed to know that there was more to immortality than servitude.

"You okay, Mira?" Lucian's weary tone was soft as a whisper.

Quiet as they were, his words snapped Mira from her thoughts. "Yeah. Why?"

"You just look…" Lucian hesitated as if unable to complete the thought.

"I'm fine. I just haven't seen the stars in so long. They're so beautiful."

Lucian glanced upwards, but his eyes didn't sparkle the way Mira had hoped. "I guess."

"Don't take them for granted. You don't know what it's like to miss them."

"I can only imagine." He forced a smile.

She couldn't be too annoyed with him. Living a life of privilege, as he had, wanting for nothing, how could she expect him to appreciate something as small yet significant as the stars shimmering in the night sky? There was a time when she too had taken them for granted. "Nice driving back there." She hoped the subject change would break the awkward silence between them.

His chest puffed with pride. "I have to admit, it was pretty exciting."

Mira smiled at the sudden change in his demeanor. She doubted he'd ever experienced anything as thrilling as their escape in his life. "I'll be honest. I had my doubts we'd make it."

"Really?" His shoulders slumped slightly.

"Three humans and one half-blind vampire being chased by trained soldiers? Think about it. The odds weren't exactly in our favor, now, were they?"

"You should give us more credit than that."

"We did it. We survived and we're still alive. That's credit enough. Don't get cocky; you'll become sloppy." She didn't mean to downplay their abilities, but being a realist, she wouldn't sugarcoat things. That wasn't the warrior way.

Lucian's jaw tightened. Clearly dissatisfied by her lack of praise, he turned away, looking out the window toward the horizon. "So, do you have an idea as to where we're going?"

"No." Sanctuary had always been a land of legend. A rumor spread among the vampires wanting to find freedom from oppression. She'd been on the road to finding it once; before she'd been captured. Back when she was just a fledgling traveling with her sire and lover, Theo. All she remembered from those days was that they'd been heading west, toward the coast. "Nor do I know what we'll do or find if we ever get there."

"Well, you're just a bright little ray of sunshine tonight, aren't you?"

"I don't like sunshine, and I'm not going to pretend we're in the clear. We've still got a lot of question marks hanging above our heads."

"We've overcome quite a lot tonight. Allow yourself to accept that."

He was right. She glanced back up to the stars for a moment and let their silvery light brighten her mood. "I'm just concerned about what we have coming up next. Good or bad."

Lucian gently squeezed Mira's arm, a small gesture of friendship and camaraderie that felt so foreign. Touching was not something she was used to, and not something she was too sure she liked.

"I've been thinking about that as well," Lucian said. "Assuming we make it, we'll be in vampire territory. You'll have to take the lead."

"One thing at a time. First we have to find it." Mira hadn't thought about what would happen when they did encounter other vampires. She'd be reasonably safe on her own, but with three humans in tow, she was traveling with her own personal buffet. Her own kind back home had become near savage over the years in captivity; what would free-range vampires be like? What did they feed on? Assuming they had survived, what had they lived off all of these long years? So many questions. So many new worries. In some respects, this newfound freedom promised to be just as problematic as captivity.

"When we do find it, we'll need to have a plan in place."

Mira took a deep breath and gazed back up at the stars, trying to use their light to help her remain positive. "Can we leave the future to the future for now? I've not seen the stars in so long. I want to enjoy this simple pleasure for the moment."

"The stars will always be there."

"Says the man who's had a lifetime to enjoy them."

Lucian sighed impatiently but did not engage her further. They rode together in silence, putting more and more miles between themselves and New Haven's Iron Gate.

CHAPTER TWO

After hours of driving through the rough terrain, Mira's lower body had all but gone numb. Desperate to get up and stretch her muscles, she pulled the large transport vehicle behind a boulder and shut down all external lights.

"What are you doing?" a sleepy Sarah called from the back of the vehicle. She gently kissed her husband, Curtis, on the forehead and stood.

The middle-aged woman appeared so frail in the dim light – just the skeleton of a person, barely clinging to existence – but Mira knew better. She may have been malnourished, but she had a strength of spirit and more than enough balls to tell a vampire off. That and her help in their escape had earned Mira's respect. The old woman shot Mira a quizzical look, and after a few moments Mira realized she'd been asked a question.

"Sorry," Mira said. "I'm a bit numb from the drive right now. Our solar battery is running low, and I need to get up and stretch a little." Legs tingling, Mira stood. Her deathly slow circulation had her feet swelling from sitting in the same position for so long. She struggled to take a few steps without wobbling.

"Are we safe?" Worry more than fatigue colored Sarah's voice. She wrapped a blanket around her shoulders and joined

Mira at the side door. "Do you want me to drive? I'm awake now."

"You'll have your turn when the sun comes up. We're hidden. I just need a few moments to get the blood flowing again before we can get moving, okay?"

Mira lifted the door and met the cool night air.

Sarah tightened the blanket around her shoulders. "Do... you want company?"

Shock momentarily stole Mira's voice. Sarah had not been the friendliest of companions, with good reason. "Sure. Follow me."

Sluggish muscles made walking more difficult than she'd expected. Mira almost toppled out of the vehicle when she stepped down to the ground.

Sarah didn't bother hiding her amusement at the gladiator's lack of grace. "Are you sure you're okay?"

If Mira could blush, her face would have been crimson with embarrassment. Great warrior she was, being felled by a simple step! But thankfully her blood didn't flow fast enough to rise to her cheeks, and the dim light hid her awkward expression. "Fine. Just more blood than normal in my system and a lot of sitting around doing nothing. Things are just moving slowly."

Sarah's cringe at the mention of blood did not go unnoticed, but Mira knew better than to press it. Humans as a general rule would rather gloss over the "vampire" part of Mira being a vampire. Sarah wasn't that bad, despite the fact that she was human, but she couldn't handle blood in any form.

"Do you think we'll find that Sanctuary place?" Sarah asked.

Mira led the way, taking her time with each step, walking around the boulder concealing their vehicle. Slowly, her blood began to circulate. After a few moments her movements became easier. "I certainly hope so. I've dreamed about that place for the better part of thirty years."

They walked in no particular direction for a little while in silence, and then suddenly Sarah blurted out, "I know I said it before, but I want you to know how much I appreciate you saving my husband."

Her continued thanks and appreciation was heartwarming. Things like that gave Mira faith in the human race. She'd done no more than she would have expected from any decent person in her situation, but for Sarah it had changed her entire viewpoint on vampires. That one act of healing her husband's wounds had erased the prejudice Sarah had been raised with. "You don't have to keep thanking me."

"Yes, I do. I would be lost without my Curtis."

"Well, you're not. You have him. Alive and well."

"Thanks to you. I can never repay you for your kindness."

"Yes, actually, you can. Remember that vampires are not all savages. Treat me and my kind as you would any other human being."

Sarah hesitated for a fraction of a second, long enough for Mira to catch her doubt.

"We're not monsters. And we were once human, like you. Raised human, like you. All that has changed is our longevity and diet."

Sarah took in a deep breath and nodded but did not say anything further. She continued to follow in Mira's direction.

Wordlessly, they continued ambling through the rocky terrain until a low rumbling sound caught Mira's attention. She held up a hand, signaling Sarah to stop.

Unsure of what exactly was making the sound, Mira didn't want to take any chances. She scanned the land, but large boulders and gnarly tree stumps blocked her from seeing too far into the distance.

The sound grew louder. Closer.

"Stay here," Mira whispered to Sarah.

She bounded to the top of a large rock and spotted something moving in the distance. Lights. A vehicle. Heading in her direction, she spotted the vehicle, a smaller transport than the one she and her companions were traveling in. Like hers, it had a roof-mounted weapon and large front windows for good visibility. Although smaller, it appeared to be built for speed, and probably carried fewer personnel.

"Can you make it back to our transport?" Mira whispered to Sarah. "We've got company."

"Not sure I know the way back. Everything looks the same around here."

Forgetting for a moment the limitations of her human companion's weak eyes, Mira wondered why Sarah couldn't just follow their tracks back to the vehicle. But, even if she did, the timing would be off. In its current location, it was well hidden. No lights, no power, and resting in the shadow of a large boulder. No, it needed to stay put and so did they. Drawing attention to their other companions would only lead to their doom.

Sensing her companion's worry, Mira jumped down to the ground. "It's okay." She attempted a comforting hand on Sarah's shoulder. "I need you to just stay put. No matter what you see or hear, just stay here and be quiet."

"What are you going to do?"

"They're after me, right? I'll take care of them. If I fail… wait until daylight and find the others. Got it?"

"I think so." Sarah's voice warbled with fear.

"You'll be fine. Just don't draw attention to yourself no matter what happens. Even if I am screaming for my life, you do not reveal yourself." Mira would have given anything for her short sword at that moment. She'd have to settle for two fists and a pair of fangs, though.

"I'll come back for you." Mira didn't wait for a response before taking off. Putting a little distance between herself and Sarah, she headed toward the oncoming transport, preparing to meet it head on.

Moving fast and following the same path she'd driven with her vehicle, Mira wondered if they had some form of electronic tracking devices homing in on them. She needed to take them out quickly, before they had a chance to get close.

Using as much supernatural speed as she could, Mira approached the vehicle and bounded on top of it, landing hard and heavy on its roof. It slammed to a halt, almost sending her over the edge, but she managed to hang on, gripping the large roof-mounted gun for dear life.

When she found her footing again, Mira stood and, with a grunt of strength, ripped the large assault-style rifle off the roof and tossed it aside.

The hatch opened under her and immediately shut.

Crouching low, she waited. They'd have to come out the side door if they wanted to get at her. Voices, two of them, argued within the belly of the beast. Mira couldn't quite make out through the metallic walls what was being said, but she understood the nature of the conversation. She had the element of surprise on her side, and they had no plan of action to deal with her.

For once it seemed she had the upper hand.

Below her a shot was fired. The bullet pierced the roof of the vehicle and her foot at the same time. She hadn't expected that.

Tears welled in her eyes as the white-hot streak of pain shot up from her foot, but she did not let out a sound. Staying perfectly still, she waited for their next move. With all the blood she'd ingested, the wound would take no time to heal.

Another shot, this one toward the rear of the vehicle, missed her completely.

The idiots were going to just shoot up their roof in the hopes of hurting her. Mira wasn't about to play that game. She leaped down and ripped the door off the side of the transport.

Inside she found three men, not just the two she'd heard. One of them was chained down to a chair, though; hardly a soldier, but he appeared to be guarded by one.

Surprise gave Mira the upper hand. She pulled out the soldier, who was wearing all black Kevlar, similar to a handler but without the recognizable insignia. She snapped his neck without a moment's hesitation.

The driver of the transport, however, wore the same black armor but with the insignia of a handler proudly displayed on his shoulder. He'd be better trained and equipped for a vampire.

He flipped a UV torch onto Mira before she could react.

The instant searing light burned her skin. She hissed and turned her head away. Blinded by the UV torch, she'd have to rely on her other senses.

Laughing. The handler was laughing, but it wasn't genuine. He was covering up something. A metallic tinkling. Shackles. The third man. The prisoner. Based on the sound, he was being unshackled.

Overpowering the forced laughter, another male voice began to simultaneously moan painfully and sling hateful gibberish.

"You want blood?" the handler asked. "Go, there she is. Take her."

Unable to focus around the harsh UV light, Mira didn't see the hulking vampire lumbering toward her, or his meaty fist on a path toward her face. The impact of it sent her to the ground.

Ears ringing and stars dancing in her vision, Mira scrambled to get up. The handler kept his UV torch trained on her, following her every movement with it, blinding her while her opponent, the vampire half-mad with rage, bore down on her like a runaway train.

He was either new or had been starved to the point of savagery. His enraged screams might have been words, but none of the garbled slurs made any sense to her. His swinging fists, however, said loud and clear he had one mission in life: the end of her existence.

Unable to see his face for that damned light in her eyes, Mira concentrated on his feet. Years of fighting in the arena had taught her much about how an opponent telegraphs his next move. This one, while certainly strong and fast, was not a well-trained fighter. His movements were predictable: lunging forward, clumsy with each swing of his fist, nearly overbalancing himself in the process. Mira caught the pattern and dipped and dodged away from two of his swings. She was avoiding getting hit but losing ground, and that damn light was still in her eyes. If she kept this up, she'd end up tiring herself out.

She needed a plan.

She needed to take out the light so she could see properly.

She needed a weapon of some kind. If only she hadn't tossed away the assault rifle. Even blind as she was, a few shots aimed in the human's direction would be enough to give her an upper hand.

A wild swing caught her off guard, connecting with her ear. The ringing soon stopped, but now she couldn't hear anything. Suddenly feeling dizzy, she stumbled for a moment, yelling in a combination of pain and frustration.

Moments longer than she hoped it would take, her balance returned along with her hearing, but she was no closer to a plan of attack for her opponent.

"This ain't the arena, slave. No one is cheering you on," the handler teased. He fired what sounded like a gun in her direction. "Quit dancing and just die already."

That's not playing fair. The handler's taunting only enraged her further. Probably his plan. Get her mad and cause her to make a mistake.

Mira dodged another hit, but this time the lumbering vampire ducked low and swiped at her feet. Not prepared, Mira almost toppled over, but she righted herself and threw her weight towards the vampire, slamming into him instead of the ground.

He clawed at her body with his meaty hands, but Mira didn't let go. She clung to him, digging her nails into his body. He wore the same simple tunic she had been issued in the prison, which was hardly what anyone could consider armor. She could rip through it with her nails if she really wanted too, but decided teeth would work so much better. Mira bit down through the thin layer of cloth and broke skin.

With a howl of pure rage, the vampire tried to pry Mira away from his chest. She wasn't giving up. She dug her teeth in deeper, letting his blood dribble down his chest and her face. Something about his blood tasted wrong. Like it was pure metal, but not the coppery metallic aftertaste she was used to. This was more intense, but she couldn't quite place the taste. Whatever it was that was making him crazy, it was in his blood, and she wanted nothing of it. She suckled at the wound and spit it right back out, draining him without the benefit of indulging herself.

The frantic pounding and strangled screams began to die down. The handler obviously took notice. He fired his gun again, and this time the bullet made connection with Mira's body, ripping through her arm.

Angry red hot metal tore through her flesh, but undeterred, she still clung to her prey, draining him as fast as she could, wearing him down.

Another shot fired, piercing her ribs. She couldn't help the painful moan that caused her to release her prey.

Weaker now, and less filled with rage, the other vampire stumbled where he stood. He finally managed a coherent sentence: "Kill me."

"Soon enough," Mira replied. "But this guy has to die first."

Another shot was fired, scraping the corner of her eye – dangerously close to a game ender. She couldn't take much more. Despite the damned light in her face, she had to do something. And against her better judgment, she headed towards the searing light. As quickly as she could, Mira leapt on the handler.

For one trained to subdue a vampire, he went down more quickly than she'd expected, but not before squeezing off a few shots straight through her chest as she pinned him to the floor of the transport. The pain was near unbearable, but Mira had dealt with so much in her time that she managed to hold on to her sanity long enough to tear off the bastard's helmet and dive at his neck. Ripping open his flesh, she drank until the pain subsided.

Then, when she had regained her composure, she lifted her head and stared into the handler's fear-filled eyes. "You've tortured your last vampire."

Before he could utter any words, Mira dove at his neck once more and ripped out his artery.

He'd bleed out in a matter of moments, and Mira watched every last second of the wretched human's life fade away. Though she loathed to end life, this one deserved it. Payback for his own actions and all the handlers who'd tortured her over the years.

The UV torch fell from his limp hand rolled away. Satisfied, she lifted herself from the dead body and turned back towards the sickly vampire.

"Who are you? Why did you attack me?"

The vampire was large, probably close to seven feet tall and built thick and sold, but at that moment, he was a blob of man rocking on the ground like a sobbing child. "I... can't... control. Ahhh it hurts. Just kill me."

Nothing about him seemed right. And though admittedly she was not familiar with every vampire in the prison, he was definitely not a gladiator. "You're new. Who made you?"

"Magistrate. I was...death sentence... prison reprieve."

His revelation stole her voice. A sick feeling churned in her stomach. Life as she knew it – or rather life for the vampires in general – would never be the same. They'd done it. The humans had found the secret to making more vampires. They'd been dangerously close when they'd stolen her blood, though she'd assumed they were still a long ways off from actually accomplishing it. But now, here was the proof; and all vampire kind would be in danger.

"Please. Kill me," the vampire begged. "It hurts... too much... pain."

Hurts? That didn't sound right at all. Unless maybe he was hungry. "You just need blood. Have what's left of the handler." She nodded to the lifeless lump.

"No. I can't."

It was then she noticed his teeth. Or lack thereof. Where his fangs were supposed to be were empty holes.

"What have they done to you?" This, Mira knew, was just the beginning of the new atrocities to be unleashed on vampire kind. They'd be slaughtered by the thousands now in the arena, and replaced endlessly by humans farmed out of the prison systems. A sick and terrible system devised by the Magistrate.

The vampire's voice trembled with pain. "When I woke up..." He took a shaky breath. "I was in the transport. Needles injected me... If I attacked you... they'd make the pain stop."

She'd tasted something familiar in his blood. Metallic and repelling. Mira darted into the transport and rummaged around. She spotted a vial next to the seat he'd been shackled to: silver nitrate. *Liquid silver. Of course. And in one so young. No wonder he was enraged.*

"Please, kill me. I don't want to live like this."

No doubt he was in agony. "I could try to give you my blood."

"I never wanted this. Please end my misery."

Mira nodded. She'd had to do this on many occasions. She was not about to make the poor man beg. This was his wish.

Without another word she knelt down in front of him, placed a hand on either side of his head, and twisted—breaking his neck—ensuring he would be unconscious. Then, with all the force she could muster, she pushed her knee into his chest for leverage and ripped his head from his torso.

Taking a moment of silence as respect for her fallen brethren, she gently placed the head in the corpse's arms. "Your pain is over."

Listening for signs of any reinforcements, Mira scaled a large rock and scanned the horizon. Nothing, not even the call of wild beasts in the distance. It was as if all of nature was taking a moment of silence for the dead.

Satisfied the threat was over, Mira rushed back to her human companion.

Sarah huddled low where she'd been left to wait. "I heard fighting."

"It's over now." Anger over what she'd just had to do soured Mira's tone. "But we might be followed. We need to get back to the transport and get moving fast. You take the day shift."

Sarah followed in Mira's wake. Both women made quick work of reaching the transport. Not bothering to wake the others, Sarah and Mira took the front seats, started up the vehicle, and took off heading west.

CHAPTER THREE

Pushing **the limits of their** vehicle's solar batteries, taking shifts, driving without stopping, they reached the coast in a couple of days. Night had fallen, and Mira was glad for the ability to step outside and stretch her legs. Hundreds of miles from where they had left, she still felt as if there were eyes watching her every move. Glancing around nervously, Mira wondered if there might actually be someone out there in the badlands, watching. They'd already been followed once. Who knew how far the Magistrate's reach went?

Something stirred within her – instinct, maybe, or just paranoia – but nervous energy had her jumping at twigs snapping under her feet. There was another sound, too – a rhythmic slapping and rushing from nearby.

Without telling the others where she was heading, Mira took a short walk toward the intriguing noises and found a sight she'd never imagined she'd in all her long years: the beach. Damage here from the great cataclysm was apparent. There was no gentle slope from the land to the beach to the water. Rocks as big as boulders bit into the land. Broken pieces of mountain lay where they'd fallen. In some places trees had been split and found ways to continue growing around their obstructions. The sea was mere steps from her rocky footpath.

Mira had never imagined such a savage and beautiful sight. Even before she'd been turned, she'd dreamed of seeing the ocean. Stories of monsters inhabiting the wastelands kept most humans from venturing too close. She never once thought she'd become one of those monsters, or that if she did, rather than be feared, she'd be enslaved for it.

Inky black water rushed up and retreated from the small shore made completely of glittering sea glass. Each beat of the water slapping the sand and then washing it away had a soothing and calming effect. And the air! Never had she smelled such a wonderful combination of salty and sweet. This place was truly wonderful, and she hoped that if Sanctuary were real, it was close by. She could certainly enjoy living near the sea.

In the distance, a wolf howled, singing to the silvery moon above, confirming what she'd been feeling. Someone else was out there, or better yet, many someones, and they had been watching her this entire time. Others soon joined in the chorus. Beautiful and melodic in their harmony, Mira understood at once that these were not normal wolves. They were like her – sentient, part human, but more. Creatures that would be feared and persecuted by the humans. But unlike her, they were and had always been free.

Remembering what Theo had told her all those years ago, Mira ran back to the vehicle and shouted, "I beg your mercy and ask for sanctuary for me and my companions." Theo had said she'd be welcomed in Sanctuary just for being a vampire, but she had to make it known that was her intention. Of course, it was more than thirty years ago that he'd said that. She could only hope the rules hadn't changed since then.

Using all the power she could muster, she repeated the phrase again, putting as much conviction in her voice as she could manage, saying it loud enough for all to hear.

Lucian's eyes tripled in size. He looked horrified and confused by Mira, fearful of what trouble she might have stirred up.

Curtis and Sarah, who'd been asleep, were suddenly not and were climbing out of the vehicle. Holding each other close, they scanned the horizon, silently mouthing, "What's going on?" to Lucian.

He couldn't provide any answers. Neither could Mira, though she was the one doing all of the shouting. She wasn't sure if what she was doing was going to work, but she had to try.

After the third time she repeated the phrase, the wolves silenced. The sudden hush was unsettling. Had she gotten through to them? Would they come? Would they be friendly?

Behind her, Lucian finally found his voice. "What exactly are you doing?"

"Asking for refuge within the borders of Sanctuary."

"From who – the wolves?"

"Yes, exactly! I'd heard all the wolves had died off, but…"

Before she could finish her sentence a lone naked man appeared from behind some large boulders and walked unabashedly toward her.

She might have been a warrior and no stranger to the sight of a naked man, but to have it so proudly displayed in front of her was hard to ignore. A smile crept across her face against her best intentions to hold it back. *Hello, Wolfman!*

The man, this wolf, was more than a treat to the eyes. Sun-bleached waves of golden hair framed a wide chiseled face. A light dusting of that same golden hair spread across his jaw and cheeks, giving him a wild and rugged look that Mira couldn't help but find utterly appealing. As handsome as his face was, it was only the tip of the iceberg. Even in the moonlit glow, it was obvious that his body was just as sun-kissed as his hair. He was pure toned muscle and firmness that was obviously not the result of hours in the training gym. He lacked the bulk and hard lines that came from intense training; instead, his was all natural, long and lean. A physique that screamed freedom. Mira could imagine long hours spent running through the forests, not to escape but just to enjoy the wind through his hair and the thrill of the hunt.

"If you're done drooling, would you mind telling me what you are doing out here" – the man sniffed at the air and immediately zeroed in on the vehicle Mira was standing in front of – "with three humans."

"Drooling?" Arrogance was not a trait Mira enjoyed, but she couldn't honestly admit that she hadn't been appreciating his naked form. "No," she lied. "Just shocked. I didn't expect… well… Never mind. My name is Mira. I'm a…"

"I know what you are. I want to know why you're here." There was no good nature in his tone, and his body language said he was ready for a fight. Tight fists and twitchy muscles were never a good sign. Mira had had enough of fighting with her own kind in the last thirty-odd years; she'd rather not have to take on a wolf now. Her hopes of peace and sanctuary were already beginning to wane.

Opting for the diplomatic approach, Mira held her hands out to show she was unarmed. She took a deep calming breath and spoke slow and clear. "We seek Sanctuary. These humans are my companions. They helped me to escape from New Haven City, behind the Iron Gate. It's possible we're still being pursued, and we beg your mercy to allow us inside."

His narrowed eyes flitted from Mira to the others cowering behind her. "Show yourselves," he demanded. "Throw down any weapons and show me your hands."

Lucian, Curtis, and Sarah stepped out from behind Mira's shadow but did not walk forward. As ordered, they all held up their hands in surrender.

"We come in peace," Mira said, still holding her tone low and calm. "These are my…" she was at a loss as to how to describe them. She knew the word she should say, but somehow found it hard to push past her lips. "They've taken care of me. Helped me to escape at great personal expense to themselves. They will be killed if they return to their city."

"They will be dinner if they enter Sanctuary." A smile broke the scowl across the wolfman's face, but it was not friendly. He snapped his jaw and mock-lunged at Lucian. "My kind would eat them alive."

Moving purely on instinct, Mira threw herself between Lucian and the wolfman. Fist raised, she snarled, "No one will touch them."

In the distance, up on the surrounding hilltops, Mira caught the whites of eyes staring down on her, other wolves silently waiting to strike. A subtle reminder that they were not alone. Seven more by Mira's quick count sat waiting for the moment to make their move. Given the circumstances, she expected no less. Wolves were pack animals; where one appeared, others would follow. And she and her companions were strangers in this land. She lowered her fists and addressed the wolfman in front of her. "We're here as refugees in need of help. Please."

"Sanctuary is a place for Otherkin, not humans," he responded, his tone dangerously quiet.

Sanctuary was real. That fact alone trumped the foreboding feeling caused by the questionable nature of the wolves surrounding them. All those years spent dreaming about it. And now she was so close. But it was for her kind only. That was exactly what she had feared; the humans wouldn't be allowed. "I can't let them be… dinner, as you so tactfully put it."

"And I cannot allow you to enter our Sanctuary with them."
He stood rigid as a statue before her, mouth set hard in a scowl
aimed more at her companions than at her.

"I'm sure there can be exceptions made. We've come so far,
risked so much." She hoped appealing to his sympathetic side
might work. If not, she'd challenge him.

"Which means what, exactly, to us? Uninvited, unwelcome,
and unnecessary. That's all you are." The wolfman scrutinized her
silently, sizing her up.

"But—"

"Well, perhaps not you. I'm sure you have some valuable
skills. As I understand it, vampires are fighters. And you are, in
some fashion, one of us. Though you stink of human."

The nice approach was not working. Mira prepared for plan
B, tightening her hands into fists at her side. Fighting might not
be her favorite pastime, but it was something she was damn good
at. And, if she remembered anything about werewolves, it was
that they were all about shows of strength. Alpha mentality and
all that.

Surprisingly, his posture relaxed. "These rules are not of my
choosing. I am only here to enforce them. And even if they could
enter Sanctuary, they would not be safe among my kind."

"I will protect them. I am a warrior." Mira stood tall, puffing
out her chest, and met the wolfman's eyes.

He held her gaze long enough to show he was not intimidat-
ed by her, but his body remained relaxed. "Beyond the danger to
their lives, the humans – no matter how much you trust them –
are forbidden to know the location of our home. I am sure you
understand why."

Mira nodded. "I know more than most why you'd want to
keep the humans away, but these ones are different." She pointed

to Lucian. "He risked his life and title to save me. And... I cannot leave them here. It's not the honorable thing to do."

"Humans have no honor and do not deserve to be honored by our kind."

"That's not true."

"I've never met an honorable one."

"How many humans have you met, then?"

"I'm not the one needing to prove my case."

"They'll die in this wilderness. I cannot leave them here." She hadn't intended to sound so desperate, but he was not backing down from his rigid stance.

"That is not my concern. If that is all, I'll be on my way. Good luck." The wolf man turned to walk away.

That was it. They'd come all this way and failed. No. There had to be some way to make this work.

"Wait. Please." Mira ran after him. "May I at least ask for an audience with your leaders?"

His jaw tightened. He let out a sigh that was more growl than breath. "You may. But they" – he jabbed a finger at the humans – "will stay here."

Mira turned to her people. "Can you make it out here for a little while?"

Lucian's face hardened. He met the wolfman's eyes straight on and, to Mira's surprise, approached them both. "We'll be a target here out in the open like this. What if the Magistrate comes looking for us?"

The wolfman shrugged and turned away from Lucian. "That is not my concern."

"Of course not," Mira whispered under her breath.

"As I said, you" – the wolfman pointed to Mira – "may enter. They may not. Work out the details among yourselves, but do it quickly. I have things to do."

His abrasive attitude and lack of assistance was beginning to grate on her nerves, but Mira had no other choice. If she had to go to a higher power to repay her companions for their good deed to her, then she'd play nice with the wolfman long enough to make her case.

"Please give me a moment," she said to the wolfman, and returned to her group. "The vehicle is a bit conspicuous. And we're not certain of its tracking capabilities. You'll have to leave it behind. Curtis, can you strip out whatever you think will be helpful?"

"I can try, but I doubt we'll find much of anything to use out here."

"We have to make due for a few days," Mira said. "Does anyone know how to hunt or fish?"

Lucian smiled. "That's something I can do. Used to hunt game in the badlands outside the city walls with my father when I was younger. I'm sure I can make an effort there."

"That's something. All you'll need is some kind of shelter for the time being." Mira turned back to the wolfman. "Is there any place they can take shelter in while I'm gone?"

"There are some rock caves up the coast a little way. They can only be reached on foot, so they should provide some protection."

Shock momentarily took her voice. That was surprisingly helpful. Maybe the wolfman wasn't so bad after all. "Better than nothing, I guess. Lucian, can you hole up there while I work things out with my people?"

"I wouldn't be so quick to call them 'your people,'" the wolfman corrected. "You may be Otherkin, like us, but you belong to the human world."

How could this man say that to her? If he knew what she'd had to endure all these years, or how close she'd come to her own end before finding him, he would never accuse her of belonging to the human world. But how could he? He'd never known anything but freedom.

"I belong to no one's world," Mira replied. "But I do seek the council of those like me. Will you take me, or will I have to find this sanctuary myself?"

"Well said, vampire." And for the first time, the wolfman gave her a true smile, one not filled with cocky arrogance or self-importance. The light of his grin reached all the way up to his amber eyes. "Yes. I'll show you the way."

"Go then. But do not be too long." Lucian's face did not betray any emotion, but Mira could hear the worry in his voice.

Curtis held tight to his wife. They said nothing, but the fear in their eyes was apparent. Lucian might be able to survive on his own out here in the badlands, but these two? Their skills were not useful for survival. They needed refuge just as much as Mira.

She'd not leave them stranded, not after all they had risked; she had to at least try to make a case for them to join her in sanctuary. "I'll be back soon. I promise you."

"I'll hold you to that." Lucian's mossy green eyes glistened with emotion. Mira understood. At first, it had been Lucian looking to gain her trust; now it was her turn to earn the same from him. And she would not let him down.

"Lead on," she said to her guide. "Let's be quick about it."

CHAPTER FOUR

Mira followed the wolfman in silence for many miles before they stopped for a break. The sun was beginning to rise and the deep blue sky was beginning to turn gray. Pale as it was, the light creeping up over the horizon began to burn her eyes. She wouldn't last long, and it appeared the wolfman had noticed. He scrambled up to the top of some large boulders and indicated for her to follow as well.

"We'll settle in these caves so you can wait out the day," the wolfman shouted down to her from his perch on the jagged rocks.

Finding her footing was proving to be more difficult than she'd thought; her broken sandals were not meant to be worn for long-distance journeys. She tossed them aside, deciding to go barefoot if they were going to continue rock climbing. "Thanks... er... what do I call you?"

He lowered a hand to help her up the last few feet. "Stryker Wyatt of the Long Fang pack."

She took the offered hand and even allowed him to pull her up to her feet. Whether her exhaustion was from the trip, scaling the side of a mountain, or some combination of them all, Mira was feeling dead on her feet. She welcomed the opportunity to rest for a little bit. "That's quite a mouthful, Stryker Wyatt Long Fang."

"Stryker is fine. And you?"

"Just call me Mira."

"What, no last name?" His face contorted in confusion. "No clan designation?"

Mira shrugged. What was in a last name anyway? "I've spent the better part of the last thirty years being called 'slave.' Mira is all I can remember of who I used to be before I was taken by the humans."

Stryker hefted a few rocks, tossing them away from a small cave opening just big enough for a few people to take shelter in. "And how is it you came to be taken by them?"

"My sire and the rest of my group were ambushed while trying to find Sanctuary." Over thirty years had passed, and still the memory of that night stung as fresh as a new wound. Theo had promised her forever when he turned her, and the humans had stolen their happily ever after. If he hadn't been so noble, trying to save her and the rest of their group, he might have made it.

A tear streamed down Mira's cheek. She turned away hoping Stryker had not seen her momentary weakness.

If he had, she couldn't tell. His tone remained just as matter of fact as before. "Many try, and fail, to reach our lands. Not just vampires. You're lucky to be seeing them now."

"You don't know the half of it," she whispered under her breath. Something about that last phrase caught her off guard. What exactly did he mean, 'not just vampires'? Werewolves she now knew were still in existence, but was there more? He'd used the word 'Otherkin' earlier on as well.

"And these humans." Stryker's voice broke through her thoughts. "Why do you cling so closely to them? What does it matter if they survive?" He pushed one final boulder near the mouth of the small cave, using it as a doorway and then indicated to Mira to enter.

"They are my…" Again she found it difficult to complete that sentence. "They helped me against all odds to escape. Without them, I wouldn't be here."

"So now that they have served their purpose, they can die in peace."

She had every right to be cold and unfeeling towards humans, after all she'd gone through, but Mira hadn't expected such cold indifference from a wolf. "How can you say such things?"

"Mira, you know what they're capable of. There are horror stories of what happens to our kind when the humans get a hold of us. You have lived it. Sure, there might be one or two good ones out there, but humanity as a whole is evil. They cannot be trusted. They'll turn on you as they have in the past."

"I refuse to believe that. Not all humans are bad."

"It's that kind of thinking that started this whole mess. When the vampires first showed themselves to the humans, they thought they could be trusted. Why do you think the wolves and the rest of the Otherkin never made that mistake? We learned from what happened to you."

Otherkin. There was that word again, but what or whom did it really refer to? She guessed the answers would come from Sanctuary. "You also never stepped up to help us, either. Countless vampire lives could have been saved if we'd had some kind of help from the rest of our kind."

"And risk exposure and persecution for all of us? No. There would be no Sanctuary today if we'd done that."

"Is this the kind of single-minded thinking I'm going to run into when we reach Sanctuary?"

"This is the only way it can be, Mira." The finality on his tone said it better than the words had.

Exasperated, Mira blew out a long breath. "Why am I bothering, then?"

"I was thinking the same thing."

"It's no wonder we can't live in peace. No one is willing to try."

"After all that has been done to you, how can you want peace?"

"Because I'm done killing. I am sick and tired of it. In the human world I'm a slave, told to kill whomever they want me to kill. I'm good at it, sure, but I hate it. You know the worst part? I had never killed a man before I was taken by the humans. I lived in peace as a vampire with my sire, taking only what I needed and leaving my donors happy and healthy."

"You can have that again inside of the sanctuary. We have donation clinics for our vampire brethren. You don't have to worry about killing anymore."

"And that sounds like heaven, but I have the small matter of my frien… my companions to worry about." She'd almost let the word slip out but caught herself.

"We're talking in circles. Let's drop the issue. You can plead your case to the council, but they will not allow it. And once you see how we live, you won't want to go back to your old way of life."

"Speaking of your way of life, tell me… What am I to expect there?"

"That is for you to find out."

"Now you're being elusive."

"I just don't want to ruin the surprise."

"Must be a real utopia, then."

"I wouldn't go that far, but compared to what you must have come from, I'd say paradise."

"And you, what do you think of it?"

"It is home."

"Then why are you so far away from home?"

"Fishing for more information, are we?"

"Just curious."

"Wolves are happiest in the open. We are best suited for patrols and sentry duty. My pack is on patrol this week. We go out for miles, running the trails, looking for any sign of human encroachment."

"And what do you do when they do encroach?"

"That's best left unsaid right now."

Mira didn't like the sound of that and suddenly worried about her companions. She'd sent them out alone on Stryker's direction.

"I need to know. We left my companions out there."

"They'll be fine. The caves they were heading for were off our patrol route."

He'd better be telling the truth. If so much as a single hair was out of place on Lucian's head when she returned, there would be hell to pay. As much as she hated killing, she'd make an exception if necessary.

Stryker must have picked up on her dark thoughts. He patted her shoulder reassuringly. "Relax. They'll be fine while we are in Sanctuary. I'm heading out to run with my pack. I'll make sure they know about our... guests."

That actually did make her feel better. "Thank you."

"Rest. When the sun sets, we'll have a bit of a climb ahead of us."

Reluctantly, Mira settled her herself against a rock. The down side to being a vampire was the pesky aversion to light. Instead of making good time and heading toward their destination, she was stuck inside, hiding in this dark dusty cave – still better accommodation than her former cell.

Stryker stood and stretched. "I'll be back to get you at sun-set." He walked outside and pushed the large boulder in front of the mouth of the cave.

Mira waved behind her without looking. "See you then." The day promised to be a long one, alone with her thoughts.

CHAPTER FIVE

S he hadn't expected to actually fall asleep, as on edge as she had been, but sheer exhaustion took over. Mira was so startled by Stryker's return she nearly took his head off with a wild swing of her arm.

"Easy there, warrior." He caught her by the wrist with surprising strength.

"What happened?" Head fuzzy with sleep, Mira tried to blink it away, but her body fought to cling to that peaceful resting state.

"I'm here to take you the rest of the way home, remember?"

"Home? What?" So foreign, that word: home. Why had he used it? Sanctuary. That was how she knew it. Home was... a dank, dark prison cell. No, that wasn't home either. Not anymore.

"Are you okay, Mira?" He dropped a small rucksack on the ground and squatted down in front of her, meeting her eyes with concern.

"So... tired. Just give me a moment or two." She must have needed that bit of sleep more than she realized. Never before had she had such trouble waking. Back in the prison, she'd been routinely jarred into consciousness and had snapped straight to attention. Why now was she fighting the fog to gain her foothold in reality?

"When was the last time you fed?"

"It's been a bit." Mira couldn't actually remember when she'd fed last. Had she fed since saving Curtis's life? That had to be it.

"C'mon. You can take some from me if you need. We've got a little bit of a climb tonight to get the rest of the way there."

Stryker unsnapped a leather bracer around his wrist. It was covered with strange, beautiful swirling symbols. It was then that she noticed he was wearing clothes. When he'd left earlier that morning, he'd still been stark naked. A sight she could certainly get used to seeing – but it wasn't practical for their trek. Now, however, he looked as if he were ready for a rough hike, though she found herself missing the eye candy. She made a mental note to ask him about the bracer later. He held out his bare wrist to her as if he'd done it many times before. Mira wondered if he was one of the donors he'd mentioned they had in Sanctuary. "Take only what you need, please. We both need our strength."

Not about to pass up an offer like that, she immediately seized his arm and bit down like a viper into the soft flesh of his wrist.

Stryker didn't flinch or utter a single sound as she drank.

He was strong. His blood tasted like pure energy and heat. Unlike anything else she'd tasted before. Even feeding from her own kind on a win did not produce the same surge of power that the wolf's blood had given her. After only a few gulps Mira was sated and ready to go. She pulled away and wiped her mouth.

"That was… amazing."

"Never had a wolf, have you?" Stryker flashed her a cocky smile. Mira noticed that even as a human, his teeth were sharp. Not enough to raise suspicion, but certainly noticeable to her.

"Honestly, I'd heard your kind all died out."

"And that's what we want the human folk to think, too."

"I'm not saying I agree with you, but I do see your reason."

"We're not going to get back into that conversation again." Stryker clamped the bracer back onto his wrist, then dug out a pair of shoes from his rucksack. "Wear these." He tossed them at her. "You'll need them for the climb."

Much better than her broken sandals, these shoes were light-weight and had a soft flexible sole with a good bit of grip on the bottom.

"Thank you," she said earnestly.

"Hurry up and get ready."

Mira quickly tossed the shoes on, dusted herself off, and took a few quick steps toward the entrance to the cave, testing the traction on the new footwear. "I'm ready. It's not like I have anything to pack. Let's go."

With Stryker leading the way, the next couple of hours were spent hiking and scrambling up through the rocky terrain to another cave.

"In here," Stryker called, and set down his rucksack.

Mira followed close, not expecting to run face to face with another person the moment she entered the mouth of the cave. "Shit, sorry." She stumbled, catching herself before falling to the ground.

"State your name, kind, and purpose here," the man, a very short one, barked at her.

A guard, Mira assumed, but not armed; at least, not in the conventional sense. She stole a quick glance at his teeth as he talked. They were not sharp at all. Not a vampire or a wolf. What kind was he? she wondered. Human, maybe? No. Not here. He was short, even by human standards. If she didn't know better, she'd call him a dwarf. But those didn't exist outside of stories... or did they? He wore a funny little feathered hat and cloak. An odd uniform, Mira thought, for a sentry.

"Name and purpose," the funny little man ordered again.

Whatever he was, he was an ass. "Mira, vampire, sanctuary." If he wanted to be rude, she'd play that game too. She gave him no more than exactly what he asked for.

His yellow-green eyes narrowed on her, scrutinizing every inch of her person.

"She checks out, Remy. Just let her pass." Stryker grasped Mira by the arm and nodded his head for her to follow.

Unwelcome touching brought up feelings of rage. Mira had only just left man-handlers like this, and she was not about to let anyone else get away with it.

The guard known as Remy reached out and grasped Mira's other arm, pulling her back. "Not so fast."

She sized up the little man grasping her right arm, noting all of his weak points, and tensed, ready to strike.

"Both of you better take your hands off of me before I rip your arms from their sockets." Sanctuary or not, Mira was not about to be manhandled by these strangers. And, fueled by the fresh blood she'd ingested, she was ready for a fight.

"Mira, relax." Stryker spoke softly, releasing her arm. "I'm the one helping you here."

Mira snarled at Remy who still held tightly to her arm. "That was your last warning." She swung her arm in a wide arc, hooking the guard's arm as she came full circle, and pulled it behind his back. "You going to let me in? Or am I going to have to re arrange your body parts?"

"Okay, okay. Just doing my job." Remy's attempt to sound angry was thwarted by the crack in his voice. Mira had been on the receiving end of that same tone on many occasions. No man liked being beaten by a girl. Still, he tried to play tough to save face. "I have to call your info in before I can let you pass. Let me go."

"You could have just said that instead of trying to take the macho route." Mira released his arm and took a step back. "What kind are you, anyway? You're obviously not a vampire... too slow. And you're not a wolf like Stryker here."

"It's rude to ask such a question." Remy's tone had become spiteful.

"You're going to school me on what is rude?" Mira had to suppress her laughter.

"I'm Otherkin. That's all you need know." The way he spoke sounded as if she'd insulted more than just his pride.

So touchy for one who was standing guard. Mira wondered how someone with such a weak nature could be in charge of watching the front gates.

"Well... Otherkin or whatever, for a guard you're pretty weak," Mira replied with equal snark.

Remy turned to Stryker. "I have to call this in. You will wait with her here." Talking to one of his own, Remy's voice regained its authoritative tone.

Stryker looked as if he wanted to slap the smirk off of Remy's face, but held back. "Do what you have to."

Remy pulled an electronic device from his pocket. Long and rectangular, completely made up of screen, like a flat version of the com-link bracers the Elites back in New Haven wore. It shouldn't, but seeing others with such technology seemed odd. She'd assumed Sanctuary wouldn't be as technologically advanced. Remy began to tap the screen, humming a soft melody as he worked.

She couldn't quite place it, but the tune was familiar to her: soft, like a lullaby. The comforting notes helped to ease Mira's tension. Her shoulders relaxed. Annoyance melted away and she sighed, releasing all the pressure she hadn't realized she'd been holding in.

Remy continued to hum while tapping away at the device in his hand, but Mira no longer felt rushed to get past him. She leaned against the cave wall, enjoying the cool stone against her skin.

Something about that melody. It sounded familiar, yet she couldn't recall the song. Something about being outside, yes. It was a song about the beauty of the night. A sudden urge hit her – the cave walls were too dark and constricting. She should step outside and enjoy that beautiful mountain scenery. Take a look at the stars she had so long missed.

Yes, this issue with Remy will take a while longer. Stepping outside and walking in the moonlight would be a better use of time.

Much calmer, Mira decided to take a peek outside and get the lay of the land.

"Where do you think you're going?" Stryker asked.

"Out," Mira replied as she began to retrace her steps back down the rocky slope.

"Get back here," Stryker yelled. "And you… Remy, stop that this instant!"

Remy's humming stopped, and he glanced up innocently. "She called me weak. I could have walked her straight off the Cliffside."

The melody left her, taking with it all the calm feelings it had brought. Mira suddenly found herself outside, wondering how the hell she had gotten there. "Someone want to tell me what is going on?"

Stryker shot a heated glare back towards the guard. "Behave, Remy, she's requested sanctuary."

"OK. Fine. She's cleared to go in." Remy held up the small device and smiled.

"Mira, get back in here. Let's go inside," Stryker shouted.

Confused and a little more annoyed, Mira scrambled back up the rocky slope into the cave. She sneered at Remy, knowing he must have had something to do with her heading back the way she'd came, but couldn't quite figure out what.

"So, are we going to leave me in the dark, or are you going to tell me what just happened?" Mira grumbled as she reached Stryker.

"Best you don't know for now." Stryker winked and held his hand out pointing the way. "Ladies first."

Secrets were not among Mira's favorite things. Remy had done something, of that she was sure, but the what and how being kept from her set her on edge. Sanctuary was starting to look just as bad as where she'd come from. She hoped it wouldn't be the case. Otherkin he called himself. Stryker had used that term before too. So they must be part human but not entirely so. How many Otherkin were there? And what were they capable of doing?

Uneasy about what else she'd find, Mira headed deeper into the cave, in the direction Stryker had pointed.

The cave was dark and smelled of mold. Even though it was night, ahead Mira expected to see light or some sign, a torch or something similar, that they were heading for an exit, but there was only darkness. Thankfully having enhanced senses, she was not walking blind. The path was murky, but she could see enough to avoid stumbling.

"How much further?" Mira asked, wondering how he was able to see where they were going. Were wolves as gifted with senses as vampires?

"Just around this last wall, and we should reach the exit."

The cave floor leveled and the passage turned sharply left, then right, then left again. After all the twisting and turning, Mira finally saw the lights she had been expecting to see. A vast city of lights lay ahead of her in a small valley below.

The sight was beyond words. Beautiful twinkling lights of blues, greens, and yellows came from small adobe-style homes. Trees and flowers and gardens were everywhere, their natural perfumes filling the air, welcoming her. In the center of the sleepy city were larger buildings with huge glass windows and domed roofs. It was unlike anything she had ever seen before in either her mortal or immortal life.

"Welcome to Caldera Grove," Stryker said proudly. "Home of the Otherkin… a refuge to all immortal kind."

The cave ended in a set of natural rock stairs that wound around the valley walls leading downward to the city below. In her excitement, Mira took them two at a time.

"Your excitement is showing. Be careful, people might think you like the place," Stryker teased.

"It's magnificent. I didn't expect to see…" Admittedly, she hadn't expected anything. Sanctuary was a myth. Even after meeting Stryker, and that horrible guard Remy, she'd still had her doubts about actually finding something other than a small settlement. This was beyond her wildest dreams, and she'd yet to step foot into the city.

"We have a thriving community here, one that has been kept secret from humans since the great cataclysm." The way he said it came across as a warning. But Mira was not going to be deterred from her task. She needed to plead her case for her friends.

"And it will remain a secret from the Iron Gate humans. Let's get moving." Mira took the lead, not knowing where she was going, and not caring either. She'd let herself get lost, if only to give her time to explore this strange and new city.

Stryker didn't attempt to alter her direction, either. Maybe he too wanted her to explore and learn about the city firsthand.

Unlike the city she'd just left, this one was not a concrete jungle. The road was hard-packed dirt, tamped down by regular foot traffic, but that was the only bit of plain dirt to be seen. Everything else was green and full of life. Like something she remembered from her own human childhood spent in the apple orchards of Pomme Meadow, but infinitely more beautiful, this place was attuned to nature. Houses lined the streets, each one having its own yard filled with trees and grass. Many of the houses were covered in lush green vines of ivy. Flowerbeds, small gardens, and pens for animals gave the outlying edges of the city a rustic and homey feel. It roused memories she'd long forgotten: memories of a simpler time without the Iron Gate breathing down her neck. Living in a farming community outside of a primary city, Mira had avoided much of the tyranny on the Iron Gate government. She'd grown up in peace and relative serenity.

Even though she was just setting foot in this place for the first time, Mira felt instantly at home. These people were very close to the land they inhabited. Just as her family had been.

As they traveled further into the city, the houses were closer and the animal pens smaller, but the green was still there. Even the quaint little shops had ivy-covered walls and small flowerboxes in the windows.

Though it was the middle of the night, the city was far from sleepy, as she had originally thought. Passersby on the streets, vampires and others, looked on at her with earnest curiosity. Mira knew why. Not only was she new here, but her attire was that of a warrior. Her ill-fitting black soldier's uniform, stolen from a dead man during her escape from New Haven, set her apart from the clean-cut, well-dressed men and women she was encountering. Her untamed hair and dirty fingernails must have made her look completely savage.

"When do we see the leaders?" Mira asked, feeling as if she might need a shower or three before actually speaking to one of these Otherkin city-dwellers.

"Soon. But before you can have an audience, you'll need to… get cleaned up a bit." There was no nice way to tell her how badly she looked, but Stryker had tried to break it to her gently.

She laughed, knowing the truth. She didn't need anyone pussyfooting around her skunk-like aroma and caked-on dirt. "You read my mind."

Relief played in Stryker's eyes. Mira suppressed the smile trying to creep across her face. He might be a big tough wolf, but underneath there was the hint of a gentle spirit.

"Come. Follow me," he said, taking the lead down a street to their left. "I'll take you to my pack's den and you can prep yourself."

CHAPTER SIX

A lthough it was unlike the highly sophisticated shower she'd experienced within the Iron Gate prison, this simple spigot of water with its gentle pressure was just as satisfying, maybe more. The water was different, somehow: softer, milder. Mira couldn't quite put her finger on it, not that it really mattered. After her long journey, the experience was simply magical. Aches and pains melted away. Her muscles relaxed, and all the tension she'd felt washed down the tiny drain at her feet. She could have stood in that shower stall all day long, but there was still the matter of pleading her case to the ruling party here in Caldera Grove. What would she say to them? Could she really convince members of this new society, with centuries of hatred, that her human companions were different and deserved entry into a sanctuary that had never before allowed it? When she thought of it that way, the task sounded impossible.

She worried for Lucian, Curtis, and Sarah waiting in caves back where she'd left them. All alone out there in the badlands, exposed and vulnerable to the elements... she hoped they were doing all right. Without them, she'd be dead; and no matter how nice this place might be, she couldn't truly enjoy it with a very real threat to their lives looming over her head. They weren't the only ones she worried for. George. The closest thing she'd had to a real friend was still back there, in the prisons. She'd promised to get him out when she escaped. Now here she was, safe in the land of sanctuary. He was still there in the prison, along with all of the other vampires like herself. And what about the Magistrate, spinning his lies, keeping the rest of humanity hating her kind, fearing them, fueling their persecution and imprisonment while experimenting on them to learn the secrets of vampire blood? Since he had apparently discovered the way to turn a human, what now? He could make an endless supply of vampires to slaughter for the human's entertainment.

She had promised to help end the Magistrate once she found Sanctuary. End his existence and find a way to save the others of her kind still imprisoned and forced to fight in the arena. All of it seemed like an impossible task. The weight of all that responsibility started a knot of tension between her shoulder blades. Not even the glorious warmth of the shower was helping to keep it from building.

"You all right in there?" Stryker called from the adjacent room, his voice piercing the roar of the rushing water. "You've been in there a while now. Just checking on you."

"Yeah...uh...fine. Just relaxing." Mira was anything but. The darkness haunting her thoughts had brought back all the tension the magical water had washed away.

"Well, hurry it up in there. I have your meeting with the council set up. They're expecting you."

No need to tell her twice. If Mira knew anything about leaders, they were very big on punctuality. She had to make the best impression possible if she wanted to gain their support. Mira hopped out of the shower, dried off, and re-dressed in a linen shirt and pair of pants Stryker had found for her. A quick run of the brush through her hair and a brown bandana to keep it out of her face, and she was ready to go.

Still looking pretty rugged but at least clean, Mira joined Stryker in the main living space of the joint pack house. "Let us hope they're in a listening mood. I have quite the story to tell."

Stryker rose from a large bean sack chair in the center of the oval room. His eyes scrutinized her, but the congenial smile did not fall from his face. "Don't get your hopes up. Be brief. Be truthful. And most of all, be respectful. Their word is law." His tone said more than his words could have. There was no hope. This was all a formality.

Mira took a deep breath. She knew this was gamble, but she had to try. No use in accepting defeat before the battle had begun. "I'll do my best. Lead on."

Back out into the city they walked, and just as before, the new sights and sounds amazed her. She'd had little exposure to what city life was like, with only her short stint in New Haven to compare it to. That place was the epitome of drab and dreary – dismal homes in a concrete jungle with hardly the tiniest bit of greenery. But here, along the streets of Caldera Grove, there was life everywhere. Plants, animals, people. Even in the dark of night, the city was alive and thriving.

They headed toward the center of the city, passing by larger and larger buildings as they moved inward. The construction too amazed Mira, large dome shapes and the use of glass and wood. Their sense of style and construction worked to allow nature inside as well as out. In the center of the city was the capital building. Its large domed roof was almost completely made of glass panels to allow in as much natural moonlight, and probably sunlight in the day, as possible. Taller by far than the other buildings around it, there was no mistaking that this was the central hub of the city.

"You'll be meeting with the ruling council there in a few moments. Prepare yourself." Stryker opened the glass panel door and waved her inside.

If intimidation was a word in Mira's vocabulary, she might have admitted to it as she entered the building. Though wide open and filled with natural light, the moment she walked inside, the ominous pressure of her task began to weigh heavily on her.

A blonde woman sat at a reception desk waiting to greet them as they strolled in. She gave Stryker an approving bat of her extremely long eyelashes and then turned her eyes on Mira. "Oh, someone new? We haven't had a newcomer in ages. And... a vampire, if I'm not mistaken."

"What gave me away?" Mira asked.

She bit her lip, probably to hold back the snarky remark she wanted to say. "Uh... you look... rugged."

Mira choked on her laughter. "I know what I look like. You don't have to sugar coat it."

"You're from that big city to the east?"

"Yeah, New Haven."

Stryker continued walking toward the elevators. "I'm going to see if the Council is ready. Mira, can you wait down here with Selene?"

That was her name. Fitting, Mira thought. She looked too exotic for a Mary or Jessica, despite her golden blonde hair. She was long. That was the only word that sprang to Mira's mind. Not just tall. Everything from her height to her hair, even her ears, had an unusual length. Elf-like, if those creatures actually existed. "Yes. Fine. Let's get this meeting over with."

Stryker nodded to Mira, but his eyes were locked with the woman he called Selene. The way he looked intently at her made him wonder if they were having some silent conversation.

She walked around the reception desk and joined Mira just as Stryker turned to disappear into the elevator.

"Is it really as bad as they say?" Selene asked.

"What do you hear of the city?" Mira was truly curious. She knew how she'd lived, but those who had lived in isolation here in this city, how could they possible know what went on?

"I only know what's in the history books. We haven't had a city-dweller ever make it to our sanctuary. Only those from the outer territories have ever made it this far."

"That doesn't answer my question. What have you heard?" She hadn't intended for it to sound so harsh, but she hated pussyfooting around a subject.

Selene's smiled faded. "One thing seems true, your lot lack manners."

"My 'lot' have been through hell and back."

"That doesn't mean you need to be rude. This is a place of peace. Do try and remember that. We're not your enemies."

"Sorry." Mira had to turn away and bite her tongue. She didn't need a lecture on manners from some prissy woman who'd probably never broken a nail, let alone someone's jaw. "Please, tell me what you know about the city."

"Really only that the city is one of the eight major cities, and the Iron Gate controls everything. Vampires are used for laborers and fighters."

"That's all true, but hardly scratches the surface of what goes on in a vampire's day to day life."

A picture on the wall behind the reception desk caught her eye: a mural depicting all manner of strange creatures surrounding a bonfire. She walked toward it, half listening to Selene's protest that she was again being rude.

"Sorry," Mira said again. "What is this?"

"I was saying, that no one knows what goes on because no one has ever escaped, but then you just rudely walked away again." She huffed like an annoyed child. Mira was beginning to dislike her; she reminded Mira of Olivia. Too self-involved to possibly care about the thoughts and feelings of others.

"Well, again, you did not answer my question. What is this paining?"

"That's the founding of Caldera Grove."

"And these creatures?" Mira pointed at some of the mural's more unique looking creatures.

"We prefer the term Otherkin."

"Otherkin, then, what manner of…" Mira was at a loss for words. She'd apparently insulted the woman and knew any other word she picked would just continue to do so.

"Mostly shifters. The mural depicts them in their half forms, so you can see and appreciate the duality of their natures."

"And the others?"

"You ask too many questions."

Mira turned and met the icy blue stare of Selene. "Can you blame me? Until a couple of days ago, this place was a myth to me."

"You're the myth. A vampire breaking free of a city behind the Iron Gate."

"Why Iron?" Mira asked. "I've often wondered that. Seems such an odd metal. Why not steel?"

Selene's lips pursed tight. Clearly Mira had hit upon something important. "You ask too many questions."

"I just think it's silly. Vampires are allergic to silver. I guess it isn't prudent to make a city wall out of that, but Iron isn't really going to stop a vampire." She hoped her innocent-sounding rambling would lead Selene to divulge whatever it was she was hiding. "I mean, what exactly were they doing with iron?"

"Otherkin are metal-sensitive," Selene practically blurted out.

"But I have no allergic reaction to iron."

"Half-breeds have lesser allergies. Natural-born Otherkin have reactions to nearly all metals, iron being the worst."

"I'm assuming I'm a half-breed then?"

"Were you born a vampire?" she asked with as much snark as Mira had ever heard in all her years.

Rather than get annoyed, Mira actually appreciated the snooty little Otherkin woman's quick-witted retort. "So what other half-breeds are out there? If I'm allowed to ask more annoying questions."

Selene took a deep breath and held it in, as if that might hold in the information she was teetering on the edge of divulging. "It's not really for me to say, but vampires and werewolves are the only two Otherkin half-breed classes."

"Fascinating." Mira wondered if she should dare press for more information.

Selene walked over to the mural and pointed down to the bottom. "See? Here are your kind and theirs. This place was founded as a sanctuary for all who were oppressed by humans."

"So the humans must have known about your kind. That's why they built the Iron Gates. It was to keep your kind out." It was all beginning to make sense, except for one small detail. "But why were the humans worried about you? They'd already enslaved my kind."

"History tells us that more than a hundred years ago, when the humans turned on our kind, they used our weaknesses to control us. Vampire kind were the easiest to enslave. Your light sensitivity was your undoing. Werewolves were destroyed by silver. The few that survived ran wild in the badlands. The rest of our kind were killed by iron poisoning. A mass exodus led by our

High Council took those that remained to the sea. It was here that we found a new home, and never looked back."

"And you just let the stragglers rot in the human prisons," Mira sneered.

"I wasn't there."

They knew all along that their kin were being tortured and killed and did nothing to save them. They turned tail and ran away, leaving those that remained to rot and die.

Selene must have seen the disdain in Mira's eyes. "Our kind would have been wiped off the face of the Earth or enslaved like you were. For the good of the race, they had to start fresh in a new land."

"Spoken like a coward. If you knew the atrocities that I've been through, you wouldn't be so dismissive." Mira tried to suppress her anger. Selene, annoying as she was, had not been the one to turn her back on the vampires. The High Council was. And she was about to meet them. Pleading her case was teetering on the edge of a lost cause, and she hadn't even begun yet. Still, though, she'd do her best.

Before Selene could respond to Mira's insult, the elevator dinged and Stryker exited through the parted doors. "They'll be ready for you in a moment. Time to head up. I trust Selene has told you all you need."

Mira did a double take. She'd assumed she was pumping Selene for information, but clearly that was not the case. This little interlude had been set up. Crafty. These Otherkin were all full of tricks. "She's told me plenty."

"Good. Set your personal feelings aside and remember: be respectful and brief." Stryker waved her toward the open elevator doors. "I wanted you to know what you were up against."

"You could have told me all of this yourself."

"No. You needed to hear it from someone with no investment in the result."

His words caught her off guard. What could he possibly mean, 'no investment?' What did it matter to him either way? Before she could put voice to her thoughts, the elevator reached the top floor.

CHAPTER SEVEN

On the ninth floor Stryker and Mira exited into a glass-domed lobby that overlooked the entire valley. The sight of it took Mira's breath away. Twinkling lights above and below her from the unobstructed sky and bustling city were a pleasant distraction.

"Wait right here," Stryker said.

Mira grunted in agreement, but didn't turn to see him ducking into a set of double doors opposite of the elevator. She could hardly take her eyes off of the beauty before her. Mira could see why they chose to stay here, apart from the humans. Not just to avoid the subjugation of her race – though why they had never gone back and fought for the survivors was an angering mystery to her – but for the human's lack of attachment to nature. It had been said that the great cataclysm was the Earth's way of fighting back against the pollution caused by her inhabitants. Never did that seem more apparent than now. Her kind, the Otherkin, remained close to Mother Earth. Living in the valley of a volcano, they managed to make a beautiful home that coexisted rather than destroyed. The humans, even all these years later, had yet to learn how to do this. Mira hoped against all hope that she could plead her case so that she would not have to leave this beautiful place. And maybe, just maybe she could find a way to bring her friend George back to experience it as well.

"Okay Mira, you're up. Good luck." Stryker spoke like a man with no hope.

And that sad fact seemed to be confirmed without words as she was ushered into a large conference room with six very official-looking sour-faced individuals.

"Allow me to introduce you to the council," Stryker said, breaking the ominous silence.

"Natasha and Michael represent the hybrid clans." Stryker indicated with his hand the pair of pale figures seated on the right side of the dais at the end of the room.

Mira acknowledged the female first. Alabaster skin and long dark hair made her look more like a doll than a living, breathing creature. She sat unnaturally still and stared back at Mira with her charcoal black eyes. She spoke no words but nodded to Mira in acknowledgement.

The male of the pair, Michael, appeared to be a little friendlier. At least his lips weren't shut tighter than a coin purse. He offered a half smile, obviously more polite than genuine. Unlike his partner, whose raven hair set off her pale skin, he was albino – platinum-blond locks straight to his shoulders, pale blue-gray eyes, and milky skin. If it weren't for the occasional rise and fall of his chest, she'd have mistaken him for a statue.

Stryker waited for Michael to acknowledge them, and after an almost imperceptible nod of his head, he continued with introductions. "Niko and Katerina represent the shifters."

Niko gazed down an unusually long and sharp nose at Mira. The way he scrutinized her, narrowing his eyes as he met hers, said he'd not be easy to win over. She matched the intensity of his stare with her own show of silent strength.

"Greetings," Katerina said, breaking the silent tension. She was a fiery redhead with streaks of sooty black in her tresses. Her smile appeared genuine and showed a mouth full of perfectly white teeth, some of which, Mira noted were quite sharp. Whatever this woman shifted into was definitely predatory in nature.

"And finally," Stryker said, indicating the last two sitting at the dais, "this is Alec and Roseanna. They represent the rest of the Otherkin."

Mira noticed immediately that Alec was shorter than the others. Dwarfish in size, but no less intimidating. He waved a dismissive hand at her and turned to his partner who was his opposite in every way. Long and slender, elfish in looks, like something Mira remembered from a fairy story when she was a child. Pixie short golden blonde hair, long pointed ears, and an air of grace that was apparent even in the way she perched on her chair. Her face held no animosity; she was peace, calm, and serene.

"A pleasure to welcome you, wayward kin," Roseanna said, her voice light and soft like the tinkling of a bell. "Not many ever make it our way, and even fewer still come from an Iron City."

"I've been told I'm the first."

"No, my dear. That would be me," Roseanna said.

Mira remembered the mural from the lobby below. There had been a tall blonde waif. Had that been Roseanna? Had she been one to make the decision to turn her back on the rest of the vampires? Rage welled within her, but Mira tried her best to rein it in.

"You were there? In the beginning, that is." Mira struggled to keep her tone conversational.

"It was I who found this place." Pride turned up Roseanna's voice.

"So then you know about the atrocities of the human city and what my kind endure."

"I know not of your plight. We were at war with the humans when I and a few refugees fled to safety."

"Excuse my ignorance, but what I know of the history speaks of no war and no Otherkin."

"History is written by the winners, my dear. When we fled, the war was over."

"Why?" Mira fisted her hands, nails biting into her flesh in an effort to keep herself calm. "Why did you flee?"

"Why does anyone flee from a fight?"

"I don't know. I never have."

"I understand you are a warrior. I am not."

That's no excuse. Mira fought hard not to let those words slip from her lips.

Roseanna's expression turned cold. "Do not judge without understanding. We were being killed by the dozens. Those humans learned every one of our weaknesses. They flaunted their knowledge of our people and our ways. They poisoned us with deadly iron and silver. For no reason at all. We had been their friends. Their allies. We helped them to survive, and this was their repayment. We had no choice but to leave."

"I'm trying to understand why you left vampires behind. If you knew what the humans would do. What they had done."

"Yours and the other vampires behind the Iron Gate bear a terrible burden. Theirs is a fate we regret, but one we cannot take blame for."

"I did not say."

"You did not have to. The truth is plainly visible in your eyes."

"I just want to understand. My people have suffered — "

"Your people's suffering is grievous, but not the reason for your presence in our city." Natasha's tone was a sharp contrast to Roseanna's, but Mira appreciated the down-to-business attitude. "State your case so we can move on to more important things."

Mira squared her shoulders and met Natasha's midnight black eyes without hesitation. She explained where she'd come from, how she'd managed to escape – thanks to Lucian, Curtis, and Sarah. No detail was spared as she made every bloody detail known.

Everyone in the room sat respectfully engaged in the story as if they were hanging on her every word. Mira had no doubt that they were. The atrocities of what she'd endured at the hands of the humans would be quite the tale for any who'd never had to live through it, especially the light box and the Magistrate's plot to create more of her kind just to slaughter in the arena.

When Mira finished, she took a breath and ended with, "I'm not asking much. Just sanctuary for me and my three human companions."

"Seems you have been through quite the ordeal." Natasha's tone, however, said she couldn't care less about the plight of anyone but herself. "But our rules are clear: No humans may be allowed inside Caldera Grove, for the protection of all."

Mira had expected as much, but wasn't about to give up. "I cannot leave them to fend for themselves, and they cannot return to New Haven City. They're fugitives."

"Might I present a solution?" the Otherkin representative, Alec, responded. He met Mira's gaze without hesitation and offered, to her surprise, a sincere smile. "Why not just turn them and be done with it? Then they would be free to join us here in our beautiful sanctuary without breaking any laws." Like Roseanna's, Alec's voice had a softness to it. Calming, soothing, easy to listen to. And despite her instinct to reject any answer other than yes, she found his suggestion held weight.

She nodded respectfully, wondering why she hadn't thought of it herself. Then, a small voice in the back of her mind pushed that thought aside and reality reared its ugly head. "But if it is not their wish, I cannot turn them against their will. That would not be the honorable thing to do."

Alec met her eyes, gazing deeply into them. His smile widened and when he spoke, his voice took on a melodic tone. "You will find, Mira, that if given the choice between life and death, a human – any creature really – will choose whatever option continues their existence."

The small fading voice of reason tried to point out the patronizing nature of his words. She herself had been forced to end a whole bunch of lives over the past thirty years in the name of survival. How could he dream of lecturing her on what creatures might do to stay alive?

But that thought, the reason and truth, was carried away on the sweet stream of Alec's hypnotic voice.

Her mind filled with warmth and acceptance. Alec was right. It really was the right option to give everyone what they wanted. In a matter of a day, they could all be happy here in Sanctuary. Why not just do it?

She found herself nodding.

Natasha's sharp tone cut through the haze in her mind. "This is our decision. If you wish them to join you, this is the only way."

Michael added, "You of course may stay here as long as you would like. But no human will cross into our borders." The tone of Michael's voice said more than his words could. This was a final decision. One not to be argued.

Both of the shifters, who'd remained silent, staring at Mira, looked to each other and nodded. "You have but one choice now. Go. Take care of business," Niko said to Mira, but his eyes were having a whole different conversation with Stryker, who'd been standing as a silent sentry next to her. She wondered what they were thinking.

"We'll be waiting to welcome you all when you return with your new fledglings." Alec's soft voice cut through the rising worry.

Yes. They'd all find their happy ending here in Sanctuary. Not the choice she'd been expected to be given, of course, but Mira had to take some small comfort in the fact they'd offered her a second option, rather than just saying no. How nice of them – Alec in particular – to offer her that alternative.

She broke eye contact with Alec and took a breath, nodding more to herself than to anyone else. A small voice whispered through the warm hazy feeling of contentment that had washed over her. Almost too low to hear, it raised some concerns. Forcing this on her companions was not going to bring about a true happy ending. Doubt began to creep back in. The alternative, though, meant they would all be left to live out their days in the badlands – a place not fit for anyone to try and survive.

"Wait, before you go," Michael said. "A word of caution. Our home has been human-free since its beginning. Should you attempt to bring them here, or divulge the location of our home, you will be held accountable and meet your final death."

His threat did not surprise her. Mira expected no less. If they did not want to turn, then she would just have to stay in the wild badlands with them. She hoped it would not come to that. "Understood," Mira said, not letting the doubt seep into her voice. She turned to leave the room without looking back.

Stryker began to follow.

"A moment please, Stryker," Niko called after him.

"Of course." Stryker turned to Mira. "Just wait outside for me, please."

Mira exited the room into the large lobby. Two towering hulks of men who hadn't been there before she entered were now standing by the door acting as sentries, preventing Mira from putting her ear to the heavy wood and hearing what was being said inside.

The warm, hazy feeling of contentment Alec's soft voice had brought now left, and all that remained was crushing emptiness, knowing what she had to do if she ever wanted to come back to this beautiful place. One more wayward glance outside to the twinkling lights made her heart ache. She didn't want to have to give this up. She'd spent so long hoping and praying to find this place, and now that she had, she might just as quickly lose it. She doubted that Lucian was going to be agreeable to turning vampire.

The moon's light gave the city an ethereal glow. Beautiful, enchanting, like something from a fairy tale. Blue-green street-lights twinkled like stars. There was magic here, no doubt about that. More than she could discover in the short while she'd been here. She could see herself enjoying living in a quaint and picturesque place like this, learning all that it had to offer. And the bonus of being around free people of her own kind was nothing short of a miracle.

The idea of turning her companions, despite their aversion, felt like it was the right choice. Once they saw this place and all of its beauty, they would think so too. And they'd have an eternity to enjoy it. Yes. They had to agree to this. They'd thank her for it in the end.

CHAPTER EIGHT

"**Leaving so soon?**" Remy teased Mira, tipping his hat as they reached the mouth of the cave.

Mira snarled at the skinny man, still wondering how the hell he could be the so-called 'guard' of the gate. She could snap him like a twig. In fact, the idea of doing just that was quite appealing. "Don't celebrate. You haven't gotten rid of me yet."

He tipped his hat again and waved her toward the mouth of the cave with enthusiasm. "Well then, let me send you off with a traveling song and wish you a merry voyage."

Before doing something she'd regret, Mira turned to Stryker. "Is there something wrong with this guy? He's on my last nerve."

"That's enough, Remy," Stryker's warning glare said more than his tone.

"Not even close," Remy replied with equal amounts of mischief in his voice. "There's plenty more where that came from."

"You do realize she's a warrior and could snap you in two before you could whistle your happy tune?" Stryker might have been joking, but his words were so close to the truth it brought a smirk to Mira's lips. She tried her best to force the errant expression away. She'd hate to give the wrong impression that she might find some entertainment in any of this.

"I could be a warrior too, ya know. Don't let this tight physique fool you. Muscles don't have to be bulky to do the job." Remy puffed out his chest and stood tall, but all it did was make him look like a crooked stick rather than a formidable foe.

"You looking for a fight, string bean?" Mira popped her knuckles and cracked her neck, loosening herself up for what was to come. "Bring it, bard."

Stryker stepped in between the two, ushering Mira out of the cave. "He's a good man, Mira. Quirky and annoying at times, but a good one to have in your corner. Let his little jokes slide, and let's get on the road to finding your friends."

"Fine. If you say so." Mira had known vampires back in the Iron Gate prison who made stupid jokes and pissed off the wrong people. They didn't last long. This Remy guy was just like them: full of attitude, but probably lacking the balls to back it up. And he was actively picking at her last nerve. He either assumed she was just some weak female, or he had a death wish. "That guy's not playing with a full deck. Perhaps too much time spent in the cave?"

"Don't be so quick to judge. Remember, to him, you are the strange one. He's usually a friendly guy. Not really sure why you two are rubbing each other the wrong way."

She scowled at Stryker. How could he put it all on her? Remy's first action toward her had been to manhandle her. Not exactly rolling out the welcome mat. "I'm not the one offering to sing a traveling song. What kind of crap is that?"

"Singing is his thing, not yours. Remember, we're all kinds of different around here. Otherkin. The name alone tells you we're not like everyone else. Try not to be so judgmental. You do want to make a life here, right?"

Yeah, very much so. Not that she'd admit her enthusiasm about it to him, but she desperately wanted to live in peace and harmony. Caldera Grove was just that. A place where her wounded soul might find peace. She sighed and let go of her annoyance at the singing fool. This was not prison. She needed to remind herself of that. There was no need to constantly intimidate those around her. "Sorry. I didn't mean to insult..."

"It's fine. Just remember that before you make any judgments." Stryker led the way down a steep rocky path.

Their descent was slow going. The terrain was unforgiving and filled with sharp dagger-like rocks just waiting to be tripped over. Mira appreciated that Caldera Grove was so well hidden. Accessible only by foot, no war machines or transports should be able to bring humans here. It was no wonder they had remained hidden for so long. Stryker bounded over large rocks and scrambled through the brush with the ease of one who'd done it many times. She guessed he could do it blindfolded. She, however, was not as nimble on the rocky terrain. Used to the flat dusty arena, she continually stubbed her toes and scraped herself along the jagged rocks.

"So, what exactly are Otherkin?" Mira asked to break the silence between them.

"I was wondering when you'd ask that. We're all gifted in some ways. Most of us are born this way, vampires and werewolves being the exception to the rule."

They reached the ground and Mira stopped to stretch. "Why is that?"

"Your kind are supernaturally gifted, but cannot pass your genes on through childbirth. You are a product of some kind of ancient magic. Shifters, muses, sirens, and all the rest of the Otherkin are born with their abilities and longevity." Stryker cautiously scanned the trees and path ahead.

The way he sniffed at the air and then bent to feel the ground reminded her of just how much an animal he was.

"So, which one are you? Werewolf or shifter?"

He shot her a look that bordered on dangerous. "Kind of a personal question, don't you think?"

Mira opened her mouth, not really knowing how to respond. She hadn't thought the question was personal; but then again, she hadn't been around other gifted people before, so she didn't really know what was considered personal. "Back in the prison, asking what fighter class a fellow gladiator belonged to was a way to brag... or in some cases intimidate." Not something to get bent out of shape over.

The scowl on Stryker's face faded. "It's okay. I was only joking. I'm a shifter. Wolf specifically. There are many kinds of shifters: wolf, bird, fish. We're able to take on one other form aside from our natural human one."

She wanted to ask what it felt like to alter your shape and become something so small and compact, but knew it might be pushing the boundaries of their tenuous companionship. Instead she smiled and started walking down a path she spotted. "That's pretty cool."

"Don't go that way." Stryker gripped her arm before the words reached Mira's ears.

Hating to be manhandled, Mira wrenched herself out of his grip. "What the hell?"

"That path is a trap."

Anger faded with understanding. "Sorry."

"We don't want anyone finding us; why would we leave a path to our door? Think about it."

"Do I want to know what perils might lie in wait down that path?"

"No human would make it alive. Let's leave it at that..."

"And what about other creatures looking for Sanctuary?" Mira wondered how many died on the road there.

"They would hopefully be found by our patrols before they stepped foot down that path."

She'd forgotten about the pack patrolling around the borders. Stryker had said he'd send them word about the humans, her companions, camping in the caves. Hopefully they were keeping a watch out.

"Lead on then." Mira waved her hand forward.

Stryker took them through the gnarliest patch of trees she'd ever seen. Her clothes, which had not been in the best of shape to begin with, wouldn't take much more. Branches were shredding her shirt to ribbons.

They walked together in silence, Stryker leading her down a path of his own. She'd never have made it alone. That was for sure. "So... do you get all the perks of your other form, too?"

"You mean smell, sight, and so on? Yeah. Even in my human form I can tell you need a bath."

Mira playfully swatted him. "Thanks."

"Look at that, a smile. I was beginning to wonder if you could do it."

"Give me a break. I haven't had much to smile about in more than thirty years."

"Understood, but now things are changing. You'll turn your friends, and they'll enjoy sanctuary in Caldera Grove with you. All will be well."

Mira stopped in her tracks. She'd left certain that turning her human companions was the right choice, but now, having given the thought time to really sink in, she wasn't so sure. "Yeah... right."

"Not having second thoughts, are you?"

Was he reading her mind, or was she that transparent? She didn't want to admit it out loud. Friendly as Stryker was, he was one of *them*, and it was in *their* best interest to keep things simple.

Turning the humans was the easiest answer, not necessarily the right one. "Just hoping Lucian, Curtis, and Sarah are okay. We've been gone from them for so long."

"It's not been that long. I'm sure they're fine."

"They're not really equipped to rough it in the woods."

"When we reach the cave, I'll leave you to rest for the day and find my pack. We can all escort you back to them and protect you while you do what needs to be done. Don't worry. All will work out. You'll see. C'mon now, we're nearly there."

Stryker sounded so sincere Mira almost believed him. But something nagged at the back of her mind – that small voice of reason. She remembered he'd been held back at the Council chambers, and wondered what instructions he might have been given. There was something suspicious about the whole thing, something that she couldn't quite put her finger on. The way Alec's suggestion seemed so perfect and the way she'd been compelled to agree. And then she remembered Remy's song, and how she had felt the same numbness and eager willingness to just walk away.

"Tell me something…"

Stryker scrambled up the side of a boulder the size of a house. "Isn't that what I've been doing this whole time?"

"I know. I'm just full of questions," Mira asked innocently. "These Otherkin. They all have special gifts, right?"

From his lofty perch he surveyed their surroundings. "Yeah, sure… talents."

"So there are shifters. And they get nifty animal abilities. Then you said sirens. What do they do?"

"They… uh… use their voices to bring people close or send them away."

"Like singing, right?"

"Yeah. Why?"

Mira remembered a story she'd read as a child: an ancient classic full of strange and beguiling creatures, one of which was able to draw a person to them with only the sound of their voice. Sirens, they were called. Though in the story they were all female. After learning of the Otherkin, she had to assume that those strange creatures she'd thought were myth had to be real. She was one after all. "Is Remy a... Siren?"

"Finally putting two and two together, eh?" Stryker laughed and hopped back down to the ground. "He makes a great gate guard. No violence needed. He can send intruders away with a song."

"I wondered about that. And Alec... what manner of creature is he?"

"It's really not polite to divulge an Otherkin's ability to a stranger."

That confirmed that they were all varied in abilities, and that Alec wasn't a siren. He didn't sing, though his voice did have unusually calming qualities. "Why is that? What harm is there in knowing what special ability he has?"

"Because... it's just up to them to tell you. That's how it works." He started on again, through the trees. "We're nearly there. Just a little bit further."

Mira sprinted to catch up to him. Even after all their walking, he was still keeping a brisk pace. "But you told me about Remy."

"No. Actually, you figured that out on your own. I had no part in that other than confirming your suspicion."

"Details, details."

"Those are the most important things. The details. If you pay attention, you'll learn much more than if you ask to have the answers handed to you."

"A philosopher and a wolf," Mira laughed.

"What can I say? I'm an old dog."

"Am I allowed to ask how old, or is that personal?"

Stryker paused for a moment, thoughtfully looking up at the moon. "I'm young enough to make mistakes, but old enough to learn from them."

Never a straight answer. "I see." She didn't bother to press the matter. Age was not something that mattered to an immortal.

They reached the cave just before the sun began to rise. Stryker left Mira inside and said he would return later.

Though she was tired, Mira found it hard to settle in for the day of sleep. Her mind raced with all that had happened. She'd gone from slave to free. She'd found the sanctuary she'd always dreamed of, and in so short a time come close to losing it. The amount of new information she'd learned in the last days had her head spinning. Mira's whole world had expanded by leaps and bounds. No more was she a ward of the government living in her dirty dingy cell, fighting for her life. Now she belonged to a new world filled with creatures she had not even known existed. She desperately wanted to remain in Caldera Grove, but worried for her human companions. Their decision would shape the future for all of them. Despite what had been said before, she would not force the decision on them. The fact that Stryker would bring his entire pack with them to help guard, more like witness, was disconcerting. She'd never fought a wolf, but prepared herself that she might have to if they pressed the matter. Honor demanded that she do anything to protect the people who had risked their lives to protect her. And, more than that, she cared about their wellbeing.

A lot was riding on the next evening, and Mira was not looking forward to it.

CHAPTER NINE

M ira awoke to the sound distant thunder. Enhanced vision couldn't help her see in the pitch-black cave. Years of being a vampire had given her an innate sense for when it was night, and she knew it would be safe to venture outside. If, that is, she could find the entrance. No light, no small sign of luminance gave her any clue which way to go. She crawled in the dirt, slowly feeling her way around for the wall, and finally located the rock blocking the entrance. With a grunt of strength, she pushed it aside.

Outside the night air thick and heavy with humidity. A long-forgotten cloying scent took hold in Mira's nose, awakening old memories. Rain. Both pungent and fresh at the same time, the smell was a reminder of simpler times.

More than thirty years had passed since she'd last known the feel of a heavy rain shower. The rain fell weekly in Pomme Meadow. Fond memories of her childhood spent dancing to the beat of the pouring rain brought a smile to her face. It had been a night dark and brooding like this when she'd met Theo.

Some might have called her a simple girl. Dirt under her nails and her raven black hair tied up in braids, Mira grew up in the fields. Her days were spent tending the land and her evenings staring up at the stars, dreaming of more excitement in her life.

Theo was the answer to her prayers. Mira literally stumbled across him, hiding among the bales of hay stored in the barn, on a night filled with stormy skies and howling winds.

Nights like that had always been Mira's favorite. She'd often take a book or three into the barn, bring a lantern, and read the night away.

Theo was like a character from her favorite adventure story. He the handsome and brave rogue hiding from persecution, and she the fair maid needing to be swept off her feet. Instead, she toppled head over heels tripping over his leg.

He caught her before her head hit the hard packed ground. "Careful now, sweetheart." His voice was deep and had a rough raspy edge to it. She looked up to thank him and met the most gorgeous pair of eyes she'd ever seen.

His icy eyes held her captive. She stared too long without saying anything, and it was he who broke the awkward silence.

"You know, they have these new things called Imagers. You could just freeze mine, put it in a frame, and stare at that all day."

"I'd much rather stare at the real thing." Even in her youth she'd never been able to slap a filter on that mouth of hers. She'd always spoke freely... whatever came to mind, consequences be damned.

"I'd let you stare at me all day, but that's when I get my beauty rest." He lifted her off the ground and dusted some of the hay off of her pants and shirt. "How about you stare for the rest of the night instead?"

"Vampire? You're a vampire, aren't you?" Mira had heard about vampires, but they were scarcely seen outside of the Iron Gate's main cities. "Are you a gladiator? Why are you here?"

"Easy there, sparky. One question at a time."

His smile was infectious. And those teeth. Deadly and intriguing all at the same time. "Sorry. I've just never met a real vampire before."

He laughed playfully, cocking his head to the side and winking at her. "Oh, so you've only met the fake kind then?"

Now it was her turn. She giggled at his joke, enjoying the laid-back way he talked. He didn't seem at all like the vampires she'd read about – cold-blooded killers who fought for sport in the arena. His easygoing nature and quick wit were a refreshing change of pace compared to the good ol' boys she was surrounded by on the farm.

"Tell me everything. I'm all ears."

"Oh, ears wouldn't be what you're all of…" His eyes traveled the length of her body. "Legs, hips, breasts."

Heat rushed up to Mira's face, turning her cheeks cherry-red as his lusty gaze settled on her chest. "Naughty boy."

"Can't help it. I love to see the blood rushing in an attractive woman. But don't let me be rude. You want to know about me. Please, come, sit. I could use the company." He made her a space next to him on the hay.

They talked for hours. Theo told her everything about his kind. He'd come from a city called Eastgate near the ocean, and had been searching for a mythical place that he called Sanctuary.

"There, the land is entirely peopled with my kind," he said. "There, I can be free to live out my days without fear of persecution. There, I can finally enjoy immortality."

"Are you a gladiator?" Mira asked, not really seeing him as the fighting type. Not that he wasn't strong enough, but his personality was certainly not that of a cold-blooded killer.

"All city captive vampires are gladiators. We're forced to do other jobs too, but primarily, our purpose in life is to entertain the masses."

"So, do I dare ask what else you had to do in the city?"

"I'd rather you not. Some things I'd rather not have to re-live."

"Sorry."

"Don't be. I'm not. I don't have to fight anymore. The arena is the worst place a person can be, but now I'm free."

"I never knew. We don't watch the games here. Too far away from the city to make the trip." Mira had planned to travel to the big city one day. She had always wanted to know what city life was like.

"Arena games are not a place for a nice girl like yourself."

"Sounds like they're not a place for a nice vampire like you."

"My looks might be nice, but I'm as ruthless as they come, sweetheart."

"Oh, yeah. I believe it all right. You're definitely hard and ruthless, like a kitten."

"Now you're just mocking me." He was on her in a moment, pinning her arms to the ground, pressing his body down on hers. "Not smart to mock a vampire." His eyes narrowed dangerously on her.

Unafraid, Mira lifted her head and kissed the tip of Theo's nose.

He couldn't hold his scowl and burst into laughter. "You're unlike any human I've ever met."

"I'll take that as a compliment."

Their connection had been instantaneous and intense. Soul-mates, if that was a thing. Mira had never been one to believe in fate or love at first sight, but they were definitely connected on some level.

"Come with me." Theo said, looking down intensely at her. "You said yourself that you've always wanted a way out. More adventure in your life. Come find Sanctuary with me."

If she'd known then where life was about to take her, she'd still have said yes. Always impulsive, Mira was the jump first, ask questions later type of girl.

And go with him she did. He turned her that very night, and after a day spent sleeping in the barn, they took off on the road to Sanctuary.

CHAPTER TEN

Mira relished those happy memories. How long had it been since she'd had a real reason to smile? Life had been quite cruel to her, the years long and hard fought. Grasping at those fading memories, Mira gazed out of the cave, looking to the thick blanket of clouds overhead. No stars could be seen, no moon, only dark angry swirls ready to dump their bounty on the rugged terrain below. A bolt of lightning arced across the sky, lighting a path as it traveled toward the ground. Seconds later the crack of thunder followed. The storm was right on top of her, and by all appearances, it was going to be one hell of a downpour.

Wolves howled in the distance. Then with another crack of lightning, she caught sight of furry beasts rushing toward her. Larger than what she'd expected, the pack moved swiftly through the trees. There had to be at least eight of them, each one different and unique in their coloration. A sooty black-footed one with a russet red coat ran next to one black as midnight, only the whites of its eyes showing in the dark. Another wolf, heather gray with black, ears ran next to a white wolf with a black mask around its eyes and over its ears. Still more wolves could be seen in the brief flashes of light. A solid brown wolf blended in with the trees, while one creamy and white camouflaged itself among the rocks. One that stood out in particular looked as if it had polka dots or a Dalmatian coat. Though their bodies were that of large wolves, there was no mistaking these were different. These had to be the other wolves in Stryker's pack.

Fat drops of water began to fall around her. A few struck her hard on the head. She turned toward the cave and waited for the wolves' arrival.

Shifting effortlessly, they changed into human forms as they entered the cave. Completely naked in front of her, Mira had a hard time finding a good place to look. With a veritable buffet of eye candy before her, she wasn't sure she wanted to avert her eyes, but she didn't want to give the wrong impression. A single female among a pack of wild dogs, vampire or not, she'd rather not create an opportunity for unnecessary drama.

Stryker brought up the rear, the large solid white wolf carrying a rucksack in his mouth. Wet from the storm, he shook dry his shaggy coat, dropped the pack, and effortlessly shifted back into his natural human form.

"Put some clothes on, you dogs, there's a lady present." Stryker gave her a knowing smirk that said he'd caught Mira looking. He kicked the pack and it fell open, dumping a pile of clothes on the ground.

Each of the men quickly took and donned their clothes, and Mira attempted to hide her disappointment. Nothing like a little eye candy to help pass the time.

"Sorry we're late. We wanted to make sure your friends were okay to ride out this storm," Stryker said, shaking more water from his hair. He pulled on a pair of shorts and found a seat by the cave wall to rest against. "Been a long, hard run tonight."

"How are they?" Mira asked, distracted by the rest of the pack pulling on their clothes, each of them a fine specimen of athleticism. No doubt the years of running wild through the forests and badlands had done their bodies well. At the very least, it appeared so. "My… companions. Have they managed to stay safe?" She blinked herself back to reality and turned to search for Stryker.

"They're holding up well. But very eager to see you return."

"You didn't tell them about what the Council said, did you?" Some part of her hoped he had. It would save her from having to break the news, and give them time to consider their options.

Resting against the wall, Stryker stretched his legs out. "No. I felt that was your news to deliver. I just let them know you were on your way back to them."

"Thanks," Mira's chest tightened. She knew stress. Fighting for her life gave her a daily dose of it, but this was different. She did not want to have to deliver the judgment to her friends. So much was riding on the decisions they would make. Not just for them, but for her as well. She couldn't leave them if they didn't agree to turn.

"We'll be holed up here for a while, boss," said one of the wolfmen, tall and skinny with a buzz cut. "Looks like this is going to be a big storm."

Another crack of thunder shattered the relative silence. Through the mouth of the cave, Mira caught sight of trees bending under the force of the wind and sheets of rain falling horizontally. Sure signs of a dangerous storm.

"Might as well make the best of it, boys," Stryker said. "Come meet our new vampire friend, Mira."

After years of being referred to by slave or by her number, hearing her name spoken by another had a wonderful ring to it. Even better, the men coming to greet her were neither armed with UV torches nor afraid to extend their hand to her. One by one, each of the men came to greet her with a friendly smile.

Terrance, Billy, Samuel, Josh, Riley, Taylor, and Rob. Each one took her hand and introduced himself.

"You guys are all from the Long Tooth Pack? That was the name, right?" Mira asked.

"Long Fang. Best shifter pack in Caldera Grove," Samuel the skinny man with the buzz cut said proudly.

"So that means there are more of you guys, right? Wolves, I mean," Mira said, sizing them up. They seemed like nice enough guys, and she loved this new feeling of camaraderie, but if her suspicions were correct, and they'd been sent to ensure her cooperation in turning the humans, she might just have to take them on. The odds were always in her favor where fights were concerned, but that was one on one. There were eight total wolves she'd have to face, if it came down to it. She needed to know more about them: their strengths and weaknesses, who else might come after her if she defeated them. Nice as this trip had been, nothing was settled yet. She couldn't let her guard down.

None of the wolves opened their mouths to answer the question. One by one, they all cast furtive glances toward their leader, silently asking what they were allowed to say – a fact Mira paid close attention to.

"We're the only pack wolves. There are plenty of other shifters, though," Stryker finally replied, after the silence had gone on long enough to become awkward.

"But I bet the wolves are the strongest, right?" Mira asked, still trying to sound friendly and conversational, although she had the feeling the pack knew better.

"You got that right!" Samuel eagerly replied.

Mira smiled. He was their weakest link. Young; no doubt his eager-to-please attitude said that loud and clear as well as his overly proud boasting. She directed her next question to him.

"So, how does the whole pack thing work? You have ranks or what?"

"Stryker's the Alpha here. Rob's the second," Samuel answered without even a moment's pause.

Yep, he was the one to press for answers.

Stryker scooted next to Mira. "You're awfully curious tonight, aren't you? Trying to find our weaknesses?" His tone clearly said he was on to her, yet he did not make any effort to stop her line of questions.

"I'm stuck her for what might be the whole night with a group of shifters. And I've never met shifters before in all my years. You can't blame me for curiosity. Aren't you curious at all about me?"

"Fair enough," Stryker agreed, "but we've been raised with vampires, so the novelty is not there."

"You're not curious about what happens to vampires in the cities?" Mira asked. Certainly they had to wonder what their brethren went through.

"You're thrown into an arena to kill each other, right?" Stryker's tone lacked any interest.

"Pretty much."

Samuel at least had the decency to show a little sympathy. "I'm sorry. That has got to be a hard life."

Mira doubted he truly understood the horrors of what she'd been through, but she appreciated his attempt at concern. "So, since you're bored with vampires, let's hear more about you wolves." Mira was glad to be able to turn the conversation back to her information collecting purposes. "You have leaders and seconds. What about the rest?"

"We do what we're told to do." Samuel was quick with the answer.

Mira leaned toward the eager wolf-pup. "And that is?"

"Our pack patrols the borders, watches the cave entrance, and guards the prisons."

"Really? You must be awfully busy. And is this your whole pack?"

For the first time, Samuel paused, as if he had misgivings about responding to this question. He looked to Stryker, who nodded before answering. "Yeah, we're small, but we can handle anything."

"I'll bet you can." Mira smiled at Samuel, but cast a quick glance to Stryker. "So, tell me about pack dynamics. How does one become an Alpha?" Mira asked.

"The strongest of us is the Alpha." This time it was Stryker who answered.

Mira gave him a coy smile. "I knew there was a reason I liked you. I appreciate a good strong opponent."

"We're opponents now?" Stryker's eyebrows knitted together in confusion.

"No. I mean, you must be a good fighter to be Alpha. As a gladiator, I can respect that. Maybe we can be sparring partners sometime."

Disbelief flashed in Stryker's amber eyes. "Haven't you had enough fighting?"

Sure, she'd had more than her fair share, but it was in her blood now. "I've been training and fighting for more than thirty years now. It's part of my life. Even living inside the peaceful walls of Caldera Grove, I'm sure I would be best suited for some kind of protection job, just to keep me sharp."

Stryker laughed. "When you become a permanent resident, then we can be sparring partners. I could use a tougher opponent than old Rob."

"Hey!" Rob, an older-looking man with streaks of silver in his dark hair, looked up. Until that time, he'd been ignoring the conversation while building a small fire. "I'll make a challenge for Alpha again if you keep that kind of talk up."

Stryker laughed heartily at his packmate's empty threat. "You want the job back, old timer, you just take it."

Mira let the information soak in. Stryker was not afraid to spar with her. He must know how strong a vampire was; that meant his strength was close enough to her own to handle taking a few punches. If her assumption were correct, Rob was the only other wolf worth fighting, and he was not strong enough anymore to hold the position of Alpha. If it came down to it, she could take them both out, and the other six might just back off. Of course, she hoped it would not come to that at all, but best to be prepared.

"Sounds like fighting words," Mira half joked, playing along with the conversation. "Back in New Haven, two opponents were sent into the arena to determine who was best. Both proud, both strong; but in the arena, only one would come back."

"That's no way to live," Rob said.

"Which is why I spent nearly thirty years trying to break out," Mira retorted. "If not for the humans I arrived with, I'd have been staked out in the city square awaiting the sun. Actually, that's where I was when we made our escape. Had spikes driven through my chest." She pointed between her small breasts, which had all of the wolves watching."

"Crispy fried vampire. What a horrible way to go!" Terrance finally piped up. He'd stayed quiet, but Mira had seen him watching the conversation unfold the whole time. A wolf who evidently had seen a few fights in his days, Terrance had a crooked nose that might have been broken one too many times and never properly set. His face too held scars, subtly covered behind a small growth of blond beard.

"Yeah, not exactly the way I had planned," Mira replied. "I'd have preferred a warrior's death, if any at all."

"Out of curiosity… aside from your award-winning personality, why were you sentenced to die?" The smirk that accompanied Stryker's words helped to dampen the insult a little.

"I outed the Magistrate in front of the whole country for trying to create new vampires."

"Outed? How?" Samuel asked.

"Arena events are televised. I spoke out in the middle of a battle about the medical experiments he'd ordered. That was after I'd spent two days having all of my blood drained from my body."

"Humans!" His voice filled with outrage, Stryker practically growled the words. "Always meddling in things they shouldn't."

"And getting away with it too. The Magistrate, no doubt, made everyone think I was just a rambling lunatic and the Regent, Lucian, my companion a traitor to the Iron Gate. It was all for naught," Mira said. "The Magistrate needs to be stopped… by more than just words."

"Hear, hear!" The rest of the wolves cheered.

Samuel slammed his fist into his free hand. "Put them on the extinct list instead of us! The whole human population!"

"Well, maybe not extinction. That's a bit rash. But at least take them down a few levels on the food chain," Mira said. "Some of those humans are decent people. If it weren't for my companions, I wouldn't be here."

Samuel shrank back against the wall like a chastised child and gazed at the fire. The whole cave took on a sad silence as the rain beat down outside.

For hours the rain poured. Lightning created a spectacular show in the sky above, and thunder cracked and rumbled so loud it felt as if the storm were trying to break open the very cave in which they were trying to take shelter. Her innate instincts told her that although the sky above was dark as night, it was now daytime and she should be taking her rest. But she'd already gotten enough of that.

Mira worried about her companions. "You think they're okay in this storm?"

A gentle hand rested on her shoulder. Mira turned to find Stryker behind her, his eyes scrutinizing hers. "They're fine. Holed up in a cave just like ours. They can weather this storm. For a vampire, especially one from New Haven, you worry an awful lot about humans."

"They're more than just humans. They risked their life for me. No one has ever done that before," Mira said. They were almost like…friends. They had risked it all to save her. They followed her out to the middle of nowhere. They trusted her to come back and deliver them to sanctuary. If they weren't friends, then who was? Why was that so hard to admit out loud?

There was understanding behind Stryker's scrutinizing gaze. Surely as Alpha, he had to understand the feeling of deep responsibility for those under your charge. "Relax." He squeezed her shoulder. "We'll see them soon enough. No one is going anywhere right now. Conserve your energy. You'll need it for the journey ahead."

CHAPTER ELEVEN

The storm raged on throughout the day. By evening, the rain had reduced to a trickle, and collectively, they decided to press on. The pack chose to travel in their wolf form. They were swift and sure-footed even over the rockiest of terrain. Mira had no trouble keeping up, and once they were out of the mountain, she was thankful to be able to move at a pace suited to her own supernatural speed.

Within a few hours they reached the cave where Curtis, Lucian, and Sarah were waiting. Mira was immensely relived to see that they were alive and relatively happy. Devastation from the recent storms was spread out before them: Freshly uprooted trees lay where they had fallen, and the ground squished under her feet, soil completely saturated by water. But despite being waterlogged, no one seemed to be any worse for it.

Lucian came out of the cave to greet Mira as soon as she was within range of his human vision. His mossy eyes lit with something that went well beyond relief.

"We wondered how long the storm might hold you up." Lucian pulled Mira close into a tight hug, holding her as if he did not want to let her go. She found this strange familiarity unnerving. Part of her enjoyed the warm embrace, his strong arms tightening around her, but another part remembered he was human, and a former slave owner. Those strong warm arms became constricting, and she felt the need to rip them out of their sockets. No. Too close. Too intimate. She needed his hands off her immediately. Pulling out of his grasp, she backed away a step. Lucian's expression turned. "Sorry. Perhaps I am a little too eager to hear your news. I lost myself."

"No. It's fine. Just not used to… hugging. I'm pleased to see you too."

Excitement faded to sadness. His expression remained flat, but the light had faded from his eyes. She wasn't sure how she'd upset him, and it seemed as if he wasn't looking at her but past her, at Stryker who'd just shifted back to his human form. She wondered if perhaps the wolves had not been as nice as promised. "We didn't want to risk travel last night, but I wasn't about to leave you out here another night. Are you well? Do you have any food or drink?"

Lucian turned toward Curtis and Sarah. "We could do with some food. I'm starving, and I know the others are as well."

Curtis stood and stretched. "Don't know if we'll have much luck finding dry wood, but I can look into getting a fire started."

"Any chance of a hunting party?" Mira asked Stryker. If she could send him and the pack away, she could learn what they'd done in her absence.

The word "hunt" clearly excited the pack, especially Stryker. His amber eyes lit up with a hungry excitement. If he were in his wolf form, she was sure his tongue would be lolling out of his mouth, salivating at the possibility of fresh meat. So very much like a wolf. "My pack knows where to go. Get on that fire and we'll bring you back something to cook over it." He shifted back to his wolf form, yipped a few times at his pack, and they all took off into the woods.

Not a moment after the wolves had left, Lucian answered her unasked question. "Stryker came by a few days ago to check on us. Said you'd been to the Council. What did they agree to?"

Not one to mince words, that was for sure. Mira had hoped to hold off on that discussion for at least a little longer, but the inevitable had to be dealt with.

"We'll get to that. Tell me. Were the wolves good to you?" Mira asked the question to Lucian and Sarah.

"They were fine," Lucian answered. "What was the Council's ruling?"

Mira stared down at Sarah. "Were they?"

She nodded sleepily. "Maybe a little rude, but they did nothing to harm us."

"Rudeness doesn't surprise me. There is no love in Sanctuary for your kind." It felt funny to Mira to refer to the humans that way.

"So then their ruling must not be in our favor." Lucian's voice fell flat. He slumped down against the cave wall. "Well, we're stuck out here. We cannot return to the city."

Mira joined Lucian and reached out awkwardly. She intended to give him a friendly pat on the shoulder, but stopped midway unsure if that would be best. "They do not allow humans under any circumstance. You can, however, go if you decided to become like me," she added matter-of-factly.

Lucian huffed. "I had a feeling it would come to that. Force us to become like you... like them. It's a smart plan, albeit not the most ethical. "

His lack of shock surprised Mira. Lucian stroked his bare chin thoughtfully. "If we turn, what awaits us there?"

"The city is beautiful. Built in the valley of a dormant volcano, it's surrounded on all sides. Fairly well protected. There are many types of supernatural creatures living together. I don't even know all the types, but they're all special."

"A beautiful city is not worth the risk of changing species. I need more than pretty trees and houses. What of our past? Will that be held against us? What of our future there?"

In truth, she had not thought to delve deeper into the deal she might be striking. She thought back to the meeting with the Council and how quickly she'd been made to agree to the option given. It was as if she'd been compelled. Damn it. Another Otherkin trick, like Remy the siren.

"Honestly, I don't know. The alternative though is life out here, for all of us. I won't go if you do not. I'll not abandon you."

That seemed to lift Lucian's spirits. "Mira, you continue to surprise me in every way. I feel terrible for the prejudices I was taught about your kind."

"Don't assign more praise than is due. I'm only doing what is honorable."

"You see? I was not raised to believe your kind had any honor."

His praise was beginning to make her feel uncomfortable. "Just like with your kind, some of us do, and some of us don't. It's not the creature, it is the individual that matters."

"I wholeheartedly agree. I wish I could say that made this decision any easier." Worry leached into Lucian's voice. "I realize I'm throwing away so much, and I cannot speak for Curtis and Sarah, but I don't want to—"

Mira interrupted him with a flippant wave of her hand. "Give yourself time to think on this. I am not here to pressure you or them. Talk among yourselves and come to the decision after you've slept on it. I will honor whatever you all choose." Mira cast a quick glance in Sarah's direction. The human female busied herself with making a fire circle.

"Will they?" Lucian said, casting a sidelong glance at the edge of the cave.

"I wonder that myself. The leader seems friendly enough, as does the rest of the group. But, they are on assignment. Before I left, Stryker was pulled into the Council chambers. If I had to guess, they're here to either ensure a quick transformation, or make sure we do not come anywhere near their territory ever again."

"You've been in once; that means you're a liability."

"The thought of a fight has already crossed my mind."

"Let's hope it does not come to that. I don't want to see any more bloodshed."

"That's probably what they're banking on as well," Mira agreed. "But what they don't know is, I am not the type of vampire to just roll over and do as I am told."

Lucian laughed. Probably the first real laugh he'd had in a while. "That'd be the understatement of the century. Part of why I liked you so much was your penchant for rule breaking. When I saw you in that hallway…"

Something loud boomed in the distance.

"That doesn't sound like thunder." Sarah ran to the mouth of the cave and peered out into the distance

Another loud crash and boom.

Mira was on her feet and heading for the mouth of the cave in moments. "No. Not thunder. Sounded to me like cannon fire."

"Cannons?" Lucian joined her at the cave entrance.

"Shhh." Mira listened carefully, and what she heard sent her heart into a fearful drumroll. It sounded like a war was breaking out. Large engine machines rumbled through the forest, knocking down trees in their path. Rapid gunfire rat-a-tat-tatted in the distance. Then came the loud boom. Targeted cannon fire aimed in their direction.

"I think turning you is the least of our concerns. The humans have found us... again."

Sarah shrieked, waking up her husband Curtis. "How did they find us all the way out here?"

"It was a trap," Lucian said calmly. "I knew they let us leave too easily. They must have tracked the transport. They knew you'd be heading for Sanctuary."

Mira's eyes grew wide. "Oh, no. Stryker. His pack. They're out there!"

"They'll know how to hide better than we do." Lucian sounded confident enough, but his voice carried an undertone of fear. "We're sitting ducks in this cave. We need to get out of here and get on the move."

Mira picked up the yelp of a wolf off in the distance and more rapid gunfire. "Doesn't sound that way to me. We... er, I need to help them. It's because of me they're in danger."

"But you just said you were willing to fight them if necessary."

Mira turned on Lucian with angry eyes. "If necessary. Exactly. Right now, they are on our side, and they need our help. I'm not going to leave them to the humans when it's because of me they are now being attacked."

"Okay, fine. We'll do what we can for them. I'm guessing the humans brought all-terrain vehicles with them. Standard procedure would dictate they send no more than three out this far. They're solar-powered, so they will have been weakened by the recent storms. If we're lucky, they might die out before we do. That would give us a chance to escape. We just need to draw their fire and keep them running as long as they have juice in their solar cells."

"Well, I'm the fastest and least likely to die, so I guess I'll run them around. You round up the wolves and bring them back to the cave. I'll take them in the wrong direction." Mira didn't give him the chance to argue; she took off out of the mouth of the cave and headed straight toward the gunfire.

Oversized armored vehicles rolled through the forest, tearing through small trees and over low rocks with ease. Large enough to accommodate three people each, they were more like tanks than the transports she and her companions had arrived in. But, contrary to what Lucian had said, she counted only two, although she kept in mind that there might be another straggler around somewhere. Perhaps it had already run out of battery. They should be so lucky.

On top of the tank-like vehicle, a man poked his head out. Wearing a standard issue black Kevlar uniform, he was probably only a regular soldier and not a handler, but that only meant that he wouldn't be carrying a UV torch. The soldier manned a roof-mounted gun and yelled something that sounded like directions to whoever was inside the vehicle below him.

She watched for a moment as he scanned the area with the large gun, ready to fire. He squeezed off a few here and there, not really aiming, probably just trying to scare up anyone or anything hiding. He hadn't spotted her yet, and she wasn't about to give him the upper hand. The vehicle came close to her position, and Mira bounded up into the tree and jumped on top of the vehicle. Surprising the gunner, she knocked him hard in the head, snapped it, and pulled the rest of his body out of the tank, tossing it aside like garbage.

She ducked down through the roof hatch into the vehicle. It was manned by only one other person, the driver. Concentrating on the buttons and levers on the control panel, he never saw what hit him. Mira was swift, ripping him from his seat, stretching his neck and sinking her teeth deep into his throbbing artery. His last dying breath came out as a strangled moan, and unlike other times, she savored this sound. She might hate to kill, but when it came to these bastards, they deserved it.

She let the drained and lifeless body fall to the floor of the vehicle. One down, who knew how many more she'd have to fell before things were finally over. At least she'd gotten to enjoy fresh blood. Being a vampire in war did have its perks.

The vehicle rumbled on without anyone at the wheel. Mira needed to do something about it before they ran off a cliff or into something else. And that gave her an idea. From the front view window, she saw the other armored tank making rounds with another soldier manning a roof gun. Time to play a little game of chase.

The control panel on the tank made no sense to her at all – levers instead of a steering wheel and an array of buttons and gauges. It seemed there was no rhyme or reason to any of it. She pulled one lever and, with an ear splitting metallic screech, the vehicle ground to a sudden halt. That wasn't what she'd wanted, but it was something she could work with. She pulled another lever and the vehicle started spinning to the right. Yet another lever had the vehicle stuttering to move. She released the first lever and the stuttering stopped, and the vehicle lurched forward. It took a bit of trial and error, but she eventually had the hang of forward and reverse, all she needed to know to turn her tank into a battering ram and set it on a course to hit the other tank.

Out the top hatch again, she rode the tank as it headed for a collision, ready to leap off and take out the inhabitants if they survived the crash.

The two tanks collided with a deafening crash, but neither tank seemed worse for wear. The man at the roof-mounted gun, however, took the brunt of the hit. His body crumpled, half in and half out of the tank's top hatch. Mira caught the satisfying crack of his ribs even through the sound of crashing metal.

She hopped aboard, pulled his listless body out of the hatch, and tossed him to the ground.

"What the hell just happened?" a man from inside the tank called back.

"I'd be more concerned with what is about to happen." Mira dove into the vehicle and answered back.

The tank lurched forward again, and the driver, a skinny male in oversized clothing, turned around and opened fire on her with his sidearm.

The bullets stung as they penetrated her skin, but they were ordinary bullets, and nothing short of a direct hit to her heart was going to stop her. She lumbered forward, turning her body at an angle to protect her heart.

"Stay back. I'm warning you!" Fear in the soldier's voice was more than evident, yet his hand remained remarkably still as he held out the gun and fired two more shots.

"I'd have let you live if you hadn't shot me, but I need to heal." Though in immeasurable pain, Mira kept her tone calm. She loved the way it invoked fear in her opponent's eyes. Nothing like cold, calculating, and silent death walking right up to you and taking its prize. "I'll be kind, though, and make it quick. So long as you put the gun down."

"No way. You can't kill me. I... I'm important. I have friends in high places." By the look of him, nothing in that statement was true. His uniform didn't even fit right. And it was a soldier's uniform. He wasn't even good enough to be special forces or a handler. She had to suppress her desire to call him out on these facts.

"Your friends are of no concern to me." His attempt was pathetic, but Mira couldn't blame him. No one wants to die. She snatched the gun from his grip and tossed it to the ground. Her teeth found the throbbing artery in his neck and ripped it open quickly.

Blood soothed away the sting, but she'd been hit too many times for one simple feeding to heal. She'd need more, soon.

The tank crashed into something, sending her and her dinner careening to the ground. Her head hit the metal control panel and everything went dark.

When she finally came to, she peeked outside. Eerie silence enveloped the forest. Her tank had run straight into a large sequoia tree. Tracks still trying to move, the tank was going nowhere. Surprisingly, the tree appeared to not even have been injured in the collision. Patterned beeping inside of the vehicle had Mira ducking back inside again.

"Report A2257. Location and status check."

Must be the third vehicle checking in. They couldn't be too far away. Mira needed to round up the rest and get as far away from this place as possible. Who knew when that other vehicle would be powered up and ready to follow?

CHAPTER TWELVE

S he raced back toward the cave, hoping Lucian had been able to get the pack together. Time was short, the sun would be up soon, and with another tank on the way toward their location, they needed to move to a new safe spot...quick.

The coppery tang of blood led Mira to the cave. Cloying and thick, the scent of it was so strong it actually sickened her. Too much had been spilled. Death was close. Surely, someone had to be dead. Muddy crimson streaks made a trail up the side of the mountain toward their cave. She knew it was going to be bad, but nothing could have prepared her for the grim scene she found when she arrived.

Of the eight pack members, only three remained standing; Stryker, Rob, and Terrance. Two more were half-shifted back into their human forms, bleeding and groaning on the ground. Three other wolves were very clearly dead, lying motionless in a bloody pile against a far wall.

Mira opened her mouth to speak, but no words came out. Three dead. She recognized Samuel, the young, eager-to-please wolf, among the dead. Just hours ago, they had all been alive and joking about what to do when Mira became a resident of Caldera Grove; and now, because of the humans, they were dead. Sadness and anger fought within her to be the controlling emotion. Those soldiers, those humans, deserved more than death. The wolves had done nothing to them, and here they lay slaughtered for being in the way. For being what they were.

"What happened with the tanks?" Lucian asked. His voice barely broke through her silent inner rage. She almost snarled at him, a human, but stopped herself when she caught sight of his face. Dirty and coated in blood, he'd apparently been through quite the ordeal himself, although he didn't appear injured.

She spotted Sarah, tending to one of the injured wolves, wrapping her shawl around his broken leg. Curtis stood like a guard next to her, watching the wolf's every motion. None of her humans were injured, of that she was thankful, but rage still bubbled inside of her. Damned Iron Gate humans and their incessant need to kill and destroy anything different from themselves!

Rob and Terrance were both tending to one injured wolf, who looked far better than the other, but still had blood matting up his creamy colored fur. Between the whimpering and yelping, Mira barely registered the man speaking to her.

"Mira, did you hear me?" Lucian asked again. "Are you okay?"

Fine. She was, but what did that matter with all the death around? Mira snarled inwardly. It took all the control she had to speak without letting the anger taint her voice. "Two tanks are disabled, but you were right, there's a third somewhere still in the forest. My guess is it will be here soon. When I left, it was calling for a report."

Hands fisted into tight balls, she took a few breaths. The three dead wolves were all she could focus on. Their blood called out to her, not to feed on, but to seek revenge for. Three completely unnecessary deaths.

Stryker approached slowly, cautiously holding his hands out where Mira could see them. "Are you okay? You're trembling."

She couldn't tear her eyes away from the three dead wolves. "Yes, trembling with rage, and I hope to be able to exercise that feeling on the third tank, if it shows up."

"We need to be on the move before then," Stryker said.

She tore her gaze away from Samuel's lifeless eyes. He was at peace now, she hoped, but she promised he'd be avenged. Mira found the same sentiment when she met Stryker's golden eyes. He too was coated in blood and bruises, but otherwise appeared to be in decent shape. Beneath the outer calm, though, smoldered a hidden fire of anger and savagery.

Their kindred hatred was a small comfort at that moment. "What of your pack?" Mira asked. "Can the injured be moved? Is there another place we can take them?"

Stryker nodded. "We're too far to make it to Sanctuary tonight, but there are some other caves we can try."

Thank the gods for the roughness of the land they lived in. The further up they went into the mountains, the less likely the humans were to follow. She doubted they'd send any flying machines out this far, but just in case, she was happy they had a network of cave systems to hide in.

"I can offer my blood to heal the injured." If it was anything like healing humans, it should be fairly quick.

Stryker nodded. "Your blood would help, but our kind heal slower. We do not have time to wait on them."

"Anything to help. I can feed them and let them heal on the road."

"Do that."

"I'll carry one of the injured while we travel, but someone else will have to pick up the other one," Mira said.

"Sure, I could carry the other, but what of our dead?" Stryker pointed to the three lifeless bodies. "I will not leave them here like this. They are my kin. My pack. We must honor their sacrifice."

This, Mira understood above all. "Absolutely. What do we need to do for them?"

"We don't have time for that," Lucian said. "I don't mean to be indelicate, but we have to think about the safety of those who remain alive."

Stryker turned an angry eye on Lucian. "We do not ever leave a wolf behind. Dead or alive. They must be carried too."

Mira sensed there might be a disagreement between the two men, something that none of them needed. She jumped in before either of them could speak again. "How far to these new caves? Can we make it to them before dawn?"

"If we leave now, maybe," Stryker said. "Same caves you slept in. They're on the way, but the terrain will be a bit rough to traverse."

It had been hard enough without the encumbrance on her last trip; carrying injured and dead would be very slow going, especially with humans in tow. No. That would not do. "What if I built a funeral pyre and held watch?" Mira asked. "You all go on ahead, and I can catch up. If the third vehicle comes by, I'll be more than happy to take care of them."

Lucian stepped forward, shaking his head. "No. You're vulnerable during the day, and that's very likely when they'll come to attack. I can't let you stay behind."

Mira laughed. While thoughtful of Lucian to think of her safety, he was in no position to actually defend her. Human as he was, he was more a liability if that other tank came calling. Still, though, he cared – and that was endearing. "I'm a big girl, Lucian. I know how to take care of myself. Even during the day."

Stryker stepped forward, inching dangerously close to Lucian. "I will stay with you, Mira. We can send the rest of the pack on ahead with the humans."

"So chivalrous." Mira let slip a small hint of a smile. It was not often a man treated her with such respect and care, and now she had two vying to be her protector.

"Don't be so quick to say that." His tone was dangerously calm. "I am under orders to make sure you are protected."

"Oh. Right. Orders." To say she was disappointed would be an understatement, but Mira wouldn't let Stryker see that. "Well, of course, you must follow orders."

Puffing out his chest, Lucian stood tall next to Mira. "Well, she's my friend. I cannot let her stay here, knowing she's in harm's way."

Stryker stepped up to Lucian, rising to his full height to look down on the human as he spoke. "First of all, Mira is a vampire. She's infinitely stronger than you. Second, she will be here with me, not alone. Together we are safer and better protected than she would be with a weak human like you."

Testosterone ran thick in the air and the looks the two men gave each other bordered on murderous. Knowing there was no love lost between humans and shifters, Mira felt obligated to step in.

She used herself as a barrier for the two men's aggressions. "It's settled then. We don't have time to argue. Lucian, you take Sarah and Curtis and go help the pack. They need you more than I do right now. Stryker and I will meet you tomorrow evening."

Lucian did not respond, but when he turned his mossy green eyes on her, she could see disappointment there.

Mira wasn't going to let that sway her. They needed to move, and fast. She went to the injured wolves one by one and fed them each a small amount of blood from her wrists. Unlike the humans, the wolves neither flinched nor shied away from her offered help.

Rob and Terrance came to help; they shouldered the injured wolves and headed for the mouth of the cave.

Lucian, still grumbling where he stood, was reluctant to leave Mira in the cave with Stryker. "Are you sure about this?"

"We'll all be reunited tomorrow night, okay? Just take care of the pack."

"She's right, Lucian," Sara spoke up, her voice weak with fatigue. "We're in no shape to fight if it comes to it. Let the two supernatural... er... people stay behind and protect our path to safety."

Curtis put a hand on Lucian's shoulder. "C'mon, Regent. Help us. These two are more than capable."

Reluctantly, Lucian grunted and went to help the other injured wolf to stand. "If you're not back by tomorrow night, I'll return. I don't like leaving anyone behind."

"You're not leaving us behind," Mira said. "We're covering your path. Now go!"

CHAPTER THIRTEEN

onstructing a funeral pyre took a few hours. The recent rains made finding suitable wood difficult, and every snap of a twig or rumble of distant thunder had Mira jumping at shadows. That third tank could show up at any moment, and with dawn growing ever closer, she'd soon become a prisoner of the elements. Together Stryker and Mira constructed a sizeable pile of wood, bark, and dried twigs. A hasty trip out to the site of the tank crash provided a few additional necessities. Mira swiped a container of oil to use as fuel, as well as a thick serrated dagger for her own protection.

They worked silently, carrying the bodies of the dead wolves down to their final resting place. Following Stryker's lead, Mira crossed Samuel's arms and legs. She gently brushed his eyelids closed with her hand and wiped the bloody matted hair from his face. She hadn't known him long. No more than a day, yet she felt his loss more terribly than that of an opponent in the arena. He'd been such an eager and friendly soul. Despite not knowing a thing about her, he had befriended her without prejudice. Even Stryker, kind as he had been, had a wall up between them. Not Samuel. So young. So innocent. Such a free spirit. He had died honorably, in battle. She whispered a promise to avenge him if she got the chance, and then backed away and let Stryker have a few moments with his fallen kin.

Stryker knelt before the pile and said a few silent words, a prayer maybe, she wasn't sure. Then, he tilted his head up, eyes locked on the moon, and let out a long mournful howl.

In his human form, she thought it odd seeing him baying at the moon, but understood that no matter his shape, the wolf must be part of him. She quietly sat back against the stump of a tree and waited for him to finish his wolf-song.

"Thanks," Stryker said solemnly as he lit the large pile of stacked wood. "You didn't have to stay behind to do this, you know."

"Yes. I did. It was the right thing to do. Don't make such a big deal of it. Let's burn these bodies and get some rest. It goes without saying that you're on first watch."

"Yes, ma'am." His tone might have been flat, but the slight glint in his eye said he truly appreciated Mira and her presence there with him on that sad evening.

Singed hair and burning flesh filled the air. Despite the revolting smell, Mira and Stryker sat as silent sentries, watching until the bodies had been completely taken by the fire. If there was anyone else out there, this was a sure enough sign to lead them straight toward Mira and Stryker.

"We should be prepared for another attack." Mira played with a long branch, waving it in the air like a sword, secretly wishing she had one at that moment. The dagger at her side would give her some help in a fight, but she'd have to be close to use it. A sword had the benefit of distance.

Stryker absently drew figures into the dirt at his feet. "I'm always prepared, but what about you?"

"I do what I have to do. I'm a warrior, remember?"

"You can't fight the sun."

"I'll fight whenever I have to." Mira threw the stick away and grabbed her newly acquired dagger. "If that means a little sunburn, so be it."

"Daggers won't help you against the sun. You can die from exposure, you do know that."

"Yes, of course I do, but I can also die from mortal wounds. Which do you think I'd prefer, going out in my sleep, or going out fighting?" Using the tip of the blade, she picked at her nails. It wasn't the nicest of weapons. Too bulky for a fighting dagger. Better suited for utility, but it would cut flesh if need be. As tough as she wanted to sound to Stryker, she did worry about what the morning might bring. Daylight was no small thing to deal with, no matter how she wanted to sugarcoat the thing.

"You know we'll be sitting ducks if that third tank does happen to come through during the day. There is too much blood, too many tracks, and not to mention this lovely bonfire to tell them we are not far."

Stryker stopped drawing in the dirt and looked up at Mira. "Or they'll think we ran off after burying our dead. Hopefully they find the booby-trapped path."

At first she thought he was randomly doodling away in the dirt, but now that she was looking at it, the squiggles and slashes resembled an ancient language. Something she'd ask him about later.

"You give the humans too much credit. They know they're tracking a vampire. They'll search caves around the area for sure."

"Way to think positively about things."

His sarcasm was not lost on her. She knew her last statement had a very suicidal tone to it. But it was the truth. After all her years of imprisonment, she had a good idea how the humans thought.

"Prepare for the worst. If it doesn't happen, great! I expected to die days ago. The fact I am still here says I've got a bit of luck on my side. Let's hope it holds up."

"Kind of a depressing way to look at things – always assuming death is around the corner, stalking you."

"I'm a realist. It's the only way to look at things. Life is going to find a way to shit on you. Best to be prepared for it."

"Or, you could hope for the best."

"Hope is for those lucky enough to live a privileged life. For people like me, hope only leads to disappointment." Though secretly, she held onto a small shred of it. Despite her penchant for welcoming death, she did not truly want it. All she ever wanted was peace and freedom.

Stryker stood and stretched. "Life's not that bad."

Easy for him to say. "Were you held in prison for thirty years fighting for your life?"

"Okay, you've got me there, but look at the friends you made. If not for them, you would still be in that prison – or worse, dead."

Mira had to bite her tongue. She knew he meant well with the optimism, but she'd lived through too much turmoil to be swayed from her stance. Arguing with him over this was pointless. "Do you know the caves well? Are there any escape routes?"

"Some are connected, and others are dead ends." Stryker smiled knowingly. "The cave we were in before has some depth to it. I'm not entirely sure where it leads, but we might be able to use it to our advantage during the daylight hours. At the very least, if we aren't found, we can keep you out of the sun."

"What are we waiting for, then? Let's go check it out."

CHAPTER FOURTEEN

Still smelling of blood, the cave gave off an ominous vibe. Stepping foot inside felt like welcoming death. And with the sun beginning to rise over the mountains to the east, Mira knew she might well be welcoming her end.

Thick and coppery, mixed with the humid mineral-laden air, the smells in the cave should have been enticing, but they only reminded Mira how easily a life could be snuffed out.

"Are you getting tired?" Stryker asked. "Most of the vampires I know start to get sleepy around this time."

Fatigue's nagging pull was definitely in the back of her mind, but anxiety kept her from relaxing enough to give into it. "Most vampires you know are not preparing to fight for their life. Sleep is probably not going to happen. I'll take first watch."

One last peek outside, before the sun had a chance to completely fill the sky, confirmed what Mira had feared: There was another tank out there. It was moving slowly, but from what her eyes could see, it was traveling in their direction. "They're out there. Let's hope they pass us by."

Stryker stepped out of the cave. Holding a hand up to his eyes, he scanned the horizon. "I'll take your word for it. I can't see anything." He shrugged and began moving boulders around the outside of the cave. "I thought you said I was going to be on first watch."

"I'm not going to get any sleep; might as well be useful." Eyes weakening with the rising sun, Mira had to turn away from her watch on the lumbering tank and retreat to the safety of the dark cave.

"You thinking about your human friends? Lucan?" Stryker asked.

Mira found it odd he'd bring up the humans at all, let alone Lucian specifically.

"I hope they made it to the cave, yes."

"He seems a bit arrogant, that Lucan."

"Lucian," Mira corrected. "Do you blame him? You kinda went all alpha male on him back there. He was just trying to be protective."

"A human protecting a vampire." Stryker laughed. "Sure – I *am* an alpha male. It's in my blood. But he engaged me first; I had to return the favor. Humans like him have an air about them. They don't respect our kind unless they are made to."

"Lucian isn't like that." She surprised herself by saying that. He was an elite, after all. "But the rest of the humans, yes." One in particular came to mind: Olivia Preston. Oh, how she'd love the chance to make her former owner, that pretty little princess, pay for all the torture she'd endured.

"You like him?"

Caught completely off guard, Mira stumbled and collapsed on the ground. "What? Who?"

"Lucian." An undertone of animosity that went beyond simple prejudice colored the way he spoke her companion's name.

"He saved me. He's showed he is an honorable man. That demands respect."

"Indeed." Stryker rolled the last few rocks near the mouth of the cave, not quite covering the entrance completely, but enough to block a majority of light. The few shafts that would make it through would be easy enough to avoid and would light the cave interior enough for Stryker to see. "And once you turn him, you can both live out your happily ever after in peace."

She'd wondered when the subject of Alec's ruling was going to come up. He'd been all too happy and helpful up until now, without even pressing the matter. But why bring it up now, and in that forlorn tone? What was going on in that wolf's head? "Do you really think now's is the time to discuss this?"

"What's to discuss? After we survive the day, you'll be reunited with… Lucian… and can turn him. Make him like you. It's your happy ending. Remember, positive thinking."

He may have covered his words with positivity, but his tone said otherwise. He was fishing for something. And rather than pussyfoot around the issue, Mira decided to meet it head on. "I do not want to turn them, and they do not want to be turned."

Stryker smiled knowingly. He slid down the wall, taking a seat in the dirt. "Did they actually say those words?"

"No, but I know Lucian's mind."

As he'd done before, Stryker began doodling in the dirt. "If they haven't voiced their denial, then the option is still on the table."

"I'm taking it off. The decision cannot be made under duress."

"That's going to be a problem." He looked up and his golden eyes scrutinized her, challenging her. He was an Alpha, one used to getting his way without opposition. She would not give him that satisfaction. But in his stern gaze there was softness too. He did not want to have to enforce his will on her, and that fact was made more evident in the soft way he said, "You have to know I was assigned to ensure you complied."

"I know. And I am prepared to defend my... humans. If I am forced to."

He broke eye contact with her and resumed doodling in the dirt. "Funny how you'll defend them to the death, but you have such a hard time calling them your friends."

"I'm working through my issues. But that's the least of my concerns." Despite trying to remain as calm outwardly as she could, Mira worried about her companions who'd gone along with the pack. What if, by some chance, the tank bypassed them and headed for their tracks instead?

"We're in a bit of a situation, aren't we?"

Mira scooted next to Stryker, watching him draw his shapes and squiggles in the ground. There was something peaceful in watching the motion of his hand. "How do you propose we remedy this... situation?"

Stryker shrugged, not looking up from his doodling. "Honestly, I don't know. I have my orders. I have to comply. That's how our society works. But, I know the situation is not so cut and dried for you and your... companions."

"You're stalling."

Stryker stopped drawing. "I am..." He sighed. "Because I don't know what to do."

She snickered silently. "And you call yourself an Alpha."

"Being an Alpha is more than just being the biggest, baddest wolf around. It's about being a leader of my pack. Making good judgments and protecting my people. "

"But you're not the leader, you're the Council's lackey."

"Hey, now. Careful what you say."

Damn her mouth. She hadn't intended to insult him. And that was a low blow, even for her. "Merely making an observation about the situation. I don't mean that you personally are a lackey. You're just blindly following orders...like a lackey." Despite her best efforts, backpedaling was not her strong suit. "What I mean is... The Council told you what to do, and now you have to do it, above what is good and right and honorable. We all risked our lives to go back and save your people... well, as many as we could."

"And that is precisely what makes this a touchy situation. The right thing to do is not exactly in line with what I was ordered to do. I know this, and I am prepared to make that case to the Council if it comes down to it."

Mira's eyebrow quirked up. "So, then, are you saying you will let us all, the humans included, reach Sanctuary without any incident?"

Stryker sighed heavily and returned to doodling in the dirt. "I'm saying we make it as far as meeting up with the group, and then we decide together what to do."

Mira had to admit, she appreciated the diplomatic way he was handling things. She was ready for a fight, and would take on the whole pack if necessary. Stryker had to know that. The fact he was not backing down as well as not immediately giving in was quite a respectable quality. "Sorry about the lackey comment. That was a low blow."

"It was."

"I just feel very protective of them. They were the first humans to ever show me kindness."

"I understand, believe me, I do. We were raised with our own prejudice against their kind. To see them act differently is strange, but gives me hope."

"They're not all good, though. Don't be fooled. I could tell you stories..."

"Oh, I'm well aware of how bad they can be."

"How? You live in Caldera Grove."

"The humans have been trying to find us for as long as I can remember. Our pack has taken many casualties defending our territory and keeping Caldera safe from prying eyes." The shapes he scrawled in the dirt became sharper. She could sense the anger transferring from his finger to the ground.

"I guess we've all suffered in some ways at their hands."

"It's a never-ending struggle."

The gentle swirls and strokes of his fingers in the dirt were mesmerizing. Mira couldn't stop herself. "Okay, I have to ask. You've been doing this all night. What are you writing?"

"It's an exercise in relaxation. An old Otherkin practice to help calm and focus the mind. Once the mind relaxes, the body will too."

"Are they words, like a spell?"

"Magic, you mean? Have I ensnared you with my drawings?" Stryker's laugh was a welcome sound after so much tension.

Mira let a small chuckle escape. "You have. I am under your spell."

"No. It's not a spell. They're just shapes. Pick five to start with and put them in random orders, not allowing the pattern to repeat or putting two of the same symbols next to each other."

"Sounds complicated."

"It's really not. You just draw whatever you feel like drawing. The idea is to let your mind wander away from what's bothering you and to focus on something relaxing. That's all."

"Well, whatever the rules, the effect is soothing to watch."

"It's become more of a habit over the years. I draw whenever I need to calm myself before a battle… or after one. I'm sure you have a similar ritual before your gladiatorial battles, right?"

Mira shrugged and fingered the dagger she'd confiscated from the tank. "I check to make sure I have a good weapon. Then prepare to use it."

That brought on more of Stryker's comforting laughter. "The simple elegance of a warrior."

"Not sure if I should be insulted or not." Mira scowled playfully.

"Take it as a compliment. We Alphas love a good warrior."

That caught Mira completely off guard. One moment he was cold and standoffish, and the next he said things like that. Then there was his not-so-veiled jealousy of Lucian. She wasn't sure what to make of the wolfman, but she had to admit, at least to herself, that she liked Stryker. He was not only a good soul, but pretty easy on the eyes as well.

"Here, let me show you how to do it. You look like you could use a bit of relaxation." Stryker scooted close to her and held out his hand "May I?"

Not normally one for touching or having her limbs manipulated, she hesitated before letting Stryker put his hands on her.

"Relax. Remember, this is the point of the exercise."

Mira took a deep breath and allowed Stryker to guide her in drawing the random shapes, creating new patterns.

For the first time in as long as she could remember, Mira felt the tension in her shoulders release. A strange feeling of warmth washed through her. She began to relax. Breathing became easier as well. The knot she didn't even realize existed in her chest loosened, and despite her initial aversion, she leaned into Stryker's body, savoring his warmth.

"You see?" He released her hand but did not back away from her body. He allowed her to lean back against his chest. "Works wonders on nerves."

Mira tilted her head back into the crook of Stryker's arm and met the warmth of his eyes. She hadn't enjoyed being this close to another person in so many years. It was as if the stresses of the outside world didn't exist anymore. "Oh, nerves are not the issue. I'm not nervous. Are you?"

"No." Stryker bent his head, his lips closing in on hers.

Their moment of peace was cut short by a rumbling engine grinding to a halt nearby. Mira picked up the sound of boots hitting the dirt. She was on her feet in a moment, trampling her beautiful doodle.

"Guess it's time."

CHAPTER FIFTEEN

Boots trampled the dirt outside of the cave – three pairs, by Mira's count. She crouched low along the farthest wall opposite the cave entrance. Stryker was up and at the ready too, just waiting for the opportunity to make a move.

"Is there another way into the cave?" Mira whispered to Stryker.

"We haven't explored the depth of this cave. It's entirely possible, yes."

She silently cursed herself for spending her time doodling in the dirt and making small talk when she could have been preparing for battle.

A face blocked one of the shafts of light streaming in from the haphazard pile of rock at the entrance. Eyes met hers, but in the darkness of the cave Mira was certain that the soldier wasn't really seeing her. Crouched low to the ground as she was, she might have been mistaken for a cave rock herself.

A soft click, one Mira recognized, echoed against the rocky walls. A shaft of blinding white light illuminated the cave. Mira flattened herself against the wall, averting her eyes, hoping to hide.

"This one looks pretty deep," the soldier called out. A moment later, a loud blast destroyed the flimsy rock barrier Stryker had created.

Blinding sunlight flooded the cave. Mira's skin began to burn. Despite the pain of it, she held her tongue. Screaming would only give their position away. But blind as she was, Mira was as good as dead if they fired another shot like that in her direction.

"C'mon." Stryker pulled her toward him and they backed further into the cave.

"What's happening?" Mira whispered.

"I think they're testing the cave. They don't know we're here yet. Stay behind me." He continued to push her back, further into the cave. It twisted, and after they rounded a corner, the light grew dim enough for Mira's skin to stop burning. Still too bright for her to see properly, she'd still have to manage with Stryker as her eyes.

More boots. Humans getting closer. Fast-paced footsteps snapping twigs and crunching the hard dirt. "They'll be armed with torches and automatic weapons," she whispered. "They're trained to shoot first."

"Good to know."

"You might be better off as a wolf. Aim low."

The boots halted. "More blood in here," a soldier, male by the sound of his deep voice, spoke out loud. "I think we found something."

"Check it quickly and let's move on. There are hundreds of caves in these mountains."

Only two voices. That was a manageable number. Mira's outlook was getting better. A fair fight here, and then Stryker could take out the final one in the tank.

Stryker stripped off his pants and pulled his shirt up over his head. He shifted into this wolf form before she could say anything and crossed to the opposite wall.

He whimpered pitifully, like a weak and injured animal. Smart man.

The light of a UV torch clicked on and shone down on Stryker, the dying wolf. He played the part well, his tail weakly moving, laying with his head between his paws.

"Looks like we found a wolf den," the soldier said.

Another UV torch clicked on. Both soldiers walked cautiously toward Stryker.

"Where's the rest of your pack?" the lead soldier asked, his voice oddly friendly.

Stryker whimpered and scooted backwards.

"Poor little guy. I wonder if that vampire made a midnight snack out of them."

"You saw the two burned bodies. I'll bet she turned on those humans who helped her. I wouldn't put it past a savage like that to kill off a wolf pack too."

Their words, while aggravating, proved exactly how wrong the humans were about her kind. The elites kept the prejudices going, painting her kind as nothing but stupid savages. And that's exactly how they treated her and her kind in the prisons. It was a damn good thing they didn't know about shifters, or they might not have fallen for Stryker's plan.

One of the soldiers knelt down to inspect the fallen wolf. The other one remained standing, his UV torch in one hand still pointing at the wolf and his gun on the other hand, cocked and ready to fire.

Mira waited for Stryker to make the first move.

The soldier reached out a cautious hand. "It's okay, little fella. I'm not going to hurt you." Before he could react, Stryker had him by the throat.

Nicely done, she thought, and took action, lunging at the other soldier. He squeezed off a shot before she could drag him down.

Stryker yelped, and the high-pitched cry said he'd been hit.

Flushed with anger, she drew her dagger and plunged it into soldier's chest, then snapped his neck in a moment and throwing his lifeless body to the ground. Frantic with worry, Mira bent and pried the other soldier off Stryker's struggling body. By the looks of it, the bullet had gone through the soldier and then hit Stryker. Blood gushed from the wolf's body. He twitched and whimpered on the ground.

"You okay? Stryker? Shift back. Tell me you're okay." She pulled the wolf into her lap, covering the gushing wound with her hands. "Tell me what to do. Can I heal you?"

Stryker didn't respond. His whimpers were fading into shallow wheezing breaths. He wasn't shifting. He was barely moving. Mira gazed down into his amber eyes. The light there was fading. She had to do something, quick.

Frantic, Mira pressed her wrist down hard onto one of his sharp canine teeth. Blood dribbled into his mouth, but he was didn't swallow. His tongue just lolled out of the side of his snout.

"Dammit. Tell me what to do! Why isn't this working?" She hadn't meant to shout, unsure of how many more soldiers might be outside of the cave, but in her frustration she was losing control.

Stryker's body was beginning to go limp.

"Oh, no, you don't," she growled. Biting her own wrist and ripping the skin away she flooded the wolf's snout with her blood.

His tongue finally moved, lapping weakly at her bloody wrist. She rolled the wolf over and fit her bleeding wrist into his mouth, letting her blood pool into his throat. Moments that felt like eternity went by before he started to wake. Whether voluntarily or involuntarily, he began to shift back to his human form.

Thank the gods! She never felt so much relief seeing the small movements and hearing the grunts of consciousness come from the half-shifted wolfman.

"On your feet. There are still more out there." Mira nervously glanced toward the mouth of the cave, the shadows playing tricks on her eyes. She could have sworn she saw a figure standing there, watching her. But no, her vision was better than that. It had to be nerves. She couldn't go out and meet the humans head-on in daylight. It would have to be Stryker.

Stryker groaned. Her blood was definitely reviving him, but more slowly than she'd hoped. He'd said they were slower to heal, but how much slower was the big question. Would he be okay to fight?

Voices on the outside of the cave sent Mira's already frantically beating heart racing. How many of them were there? Surely the tank only held three at the maximum.

They were getting closer, no doubt heading into the cave after their fallen companions. Stryker's breathing had regulated, and he had completed shifting, but still he refused to move.

Mira lifted him into her arms and stood. A quick glance around the dark cave didn't show her any other way out. No hope of retreating further into the depths either. The walls appeared solid all around. If there was another way in or out, it was hidden well from view. She took Stryker back as far as the cave would let her and set him down against the wall. "If you can hear me, stay here."

Following the wall around, she headed back towards the entrance of the cave, careful to stay away from the light.

The voices outside of the cave had ceased, but near-silent footsteps told her that they were still heading in her direction.

She waited, crouched low against the wall, ready to strike. A lip of rocks blocked her from the light and shielded her from view.

Sour sweat and dirt, the smells of a long ride with no shower, hit her nose before she saw the man walk past her. The soldier was armed with the standard issue UV torch and sidearm, which he held out cocked and ready to fire.

Mira listened, but didn't hear anything else – no other soldiers coming inside. Confident in that fact, she lunged forward and grabbed the man around the neck. He fired his weapon at the cave wall and fumbled with his torch, trying to aim it at her. "Couldn't just leave us alone, could you?" she growled in his ear. This one she would kill slowly. Take his blood to heal her of what she'd fed to Stryker.

Mira bent the soldier's head sideways, savoring the slight tremble he gave her before she sank her teeth in to his hot flesh.

Blood flooded her mouth, hot and sweet. Just what she needed. The soldier's heart pumped frantically, gushing blood so fast she had to gulp to keep from wasting it.

In her gluttony she didn't hear the other soldier coming up behind her, or the cocking of his gun. She felt the shot, though; it seared through her flesh. One shot, two, three in rapid succession. Before she could drop her prey and turn on her attacker, he'd unloaded the entire clip into her body. She was on the ground, her blood spilling out onto the dirt.

A UV torch clicked on and white hot light flooded her vision.

She spewed out every obscenity in her arsenal, both to curse herself for not being watchful for more soldiers and to put sound to the pain she was feeling.

"Gotcha now, leech!" the soldier taunted her.

"Then why haven't you put a bullet through my heart?" Mira answered back, voice filled with hatred.

"Magistrate wants you back alive, so he can personally kill you in the arena. Pity. I'd love to put a bullet between those pretty blue eyes myself."

"Then do it, you coward." Mira spat at him.

The soldier flashed the UV torch right at her face, singeing her eyes. Limbs weak with blood loss, she couldn't manage the strength to lift her hand to block the light. Closing her eyes didn't help much either. Every inch of skin the light touched burned. Mira grit her teeth, letting out a silent growl.

"I've got the leech here. She took out Watson and Briggs. Bring up the body bags and a set of silver cuffs. We'll get her locked and loaded." The soldier had to be talking through a com-link. There was still one more human out there.

"Nice work, Littleton. We'll get a promotion for sure, bringing her back."

If she wasn't in so much pain, Mira might have laughed at their atta boys. Bringing in the big bad vampire and getting a reward. How quaint.

Littleton turned off the UV torch but held it straight at Mira. "Be a good girl and stay still, and we won't have any trouble, you hear me?"

She refused to answer. Not that she could move if she wanted to.

"What. No snarky comment? The warrior rendered speechless?"

Vision fading, she struggled to keep her eyes open. Too much blood gone. At least she'd find some peace soon. Unconsciousness had its perks.

"I really did a number on you, didn't I?" Littleton smiled. "Bet you couldn't move now even if you wanted to, eh?" He kicked her in her side.

Mira barely felt it, her nerves already flooded past the point they could register. She didn't have the voice to protest, either.

"Might as well make the most of our time together, eh? Never could afford to be a patron, but I've always wondered what it would be like to have a vampire." Littleton crouched low and ran his hands up her bloody shirt, ripping it open and exposing her breasts.

Not even the rage inside of her could force her limbs to move. Of all the insults to injury, to have this oaf of a human male pawing her while she was a prisoner in her own body!

Mira prayed that her heart would finally give out and she would not have to endure more.

Littleton stood and unzipped his black trousers, smiling wickedly down at her.

As the pants slipped down his legs, she caught sight of fur. Wolf fur. She couldn't see what happened from her vantage point, but a moment later, Littleton was on the floor. Blood sprayed across her face. Littleton screamed, but it was cut short into a bloody gurgle.

Her world faded to darkness. She wanted to warn Stryker about the other human on his way in, but couldn't voice it. He disappeared from view, and unnerving silence filled the void. Did he know? Had he heard the com-link conversation? She could only hope. For his sake. Injured as he was, she didn't want him caught unawares

Everything darkened, and finally, blissful unconsciousness took Mira.

CHAPTER SIXTEEN

S weet warm liquid filled her mouth. Dark and rich, with hints of cocoa. It tingled on her tongue like little sparks of electricity. She swallowed, an involuntary reaction that sent that electricity coursing through her body. Alive and vital, it roused her from the depths of the abyss. Reluctantly, she followed the nagging sensation, waking her from peaceful unconsciousness.

"That's right. Nice and easy." Stryker's smooth voice greeted her as her eyes opened.

"Soldiers. More of them," Mira gurgled.

"Relax. Slow down. It's okay. I got them." Despite a very nasty looking black eye and an angry purple bruise on his chest, Stryker didn't look too badly off.

Mira sat up a little faster than she should have, and the sudden movement sent her head spinning. She had to put her hands out on the ground to stop herself from toppling over. Weak from her injuries and sore, every muscle in her body protested movement.

"You just can't listen to anything anyone else tells you, can you?" Stryker laughed and held a hand out to steady her.

Her mind raced a mile a minute. She'd been unconscious. That much she knew, but what had happened between her passing out and now? The gun. Her dagger. Where had it all gone? The soldiers – had they retreated, or were they still a threat? Was it still daylight? Was it still the same day? Had they missed another nightfall? She needed to get out. Been cooped up for too long. "How long have I been out for? Whose blood did I drink? The soldiers—?"

Stryker was a calm contrast to her frantic questioning. "Couple hours, my blood, and dead. Are you satisfied?"

Mira looked around. All traces of the soldiers were gone – all except for some bloodstains. The humans' blood now joined the blood staining the ground from the wolves who had died the evening prior. This cave was death. She needed to get out of it.

"When can we leave?" Mira asked.

"Sunset is close. We'll go as soon as we can. Take this time to relax."

Relax? Did she even know the meaning of the word? No, relaxing was not going to happen. If anything, she was more tense now than ever before. Hours lost and defeated by the humans. She was a gladiator; she was supposed to be better than that. She'd allowed herself to get sloppy, and look what it had gotten her. Embarrassed and humiliated, she would have been dead if not for Stryker.

Still a little weak, Mira pushed herself up and stood.

"Easy there." Stryker was on his feet, pulling her arm around his shoulder before she could protest. "You need to take it slow. You were injured pretty badly. I thought you'd died for sure, as much blood as you lost."

She saw the angry purple bruises staining his skin. He looked pretty bad himself. His legs too were a bit beaten, at least what she could see of them. Long shorts covered above his knees, but his shins carried some scars and one very nasty gash. "I've been through worse. You're bleeding. Do you need more of my blood?"

"I'm fine." He glanced down at his leg and shrugged. The wound was scabbed over already. "You don't have to be a tough guy."

George had said the same thing to her back in the prison. And she'd give Stryker the same answer: "Being weak gets you killed." And being sloppy as she'd been did too. How could she have let herself make such a fatal mistake?

"Being stupid gets you killed. So quit it and sit down. Conserve your energy, and I'll let you have more blood. You need it more than I do. You're the one who needs to be on top of your game when we meet back up with the others. Understand?"

His tone – the command in his voice screamed "Alpha," and despite her hatred of being told what to do, she listened. "Sorry. I'm used to having—"

"I know. You've had it rough. I can't even begin to understand what survival has been like for you, but you're going to have to let that guard down with me. You can trust me. I've got your back."

"Until you're ordered to kill me later for bringing humans to Sanctuary."

"I will make you this promise: I will not be the one to take any action against you. No matter what the verdict is. You have my respect and trust. You've earned that. I am your ally from here on out."

It wasn't a promise that all would be well, but his companionship reassured her in ways she couldn't quite understand herself. "Okay."

Against her own instincts, she relaxed and sat back on the ground.

Stryker held his arm out in offering to her. An angry red slash, still moist with fresh blood, ruined the perfection of his tanned skin. "Drink what you need."

Not one to turn away fresh blood, she snatched up his offered arm and bit down quickly. There it was, that dark, rich taste. Never before had she savored such wonderfully vital blood. There was an electricity to it. She could feel the energy of it reaching all throughout her body Even when she was able to taste human blood, it couldn't compare. Just a few quick gulps and she was more than sated.

"You taste amazing," she practically moaned as the high rushed straight to her head.

Stryker scrunched up his face in confusion. "Thanks… I think."

"Sorry, I just never get fresh…" After seeing the uncomfortable twist his smile took, she decided it was best not to continue the conversation. Not everyone was comfortable talking about blood. "Thanks."

"We've got about an hour, maybe two, before we can head out. Take a breather. We'll make a quick run of it once we can leave.

"What did you do with the final soldier?"

"Nothing special. A wolf isn't a threat to them. So I was able to get nice and close before ripping out his throat." He spoke nonchalantly, but the slight quirk up of his lip said he was rather impressed with himself. Mira was too.

"Stupid humans."

He snickered silently, drawing shapes below him in the dirt.

Involuntarily, she began to doodle in the dirt as well, letting the process of drawing little shapes and patterns help take her mind away from everything that had happened. They'd been through so much and still they had to face the Council. Death had already been threatened if she returned with humans. Despite her best efforts, the little Otherkin trick was not easing away all of the worry. Her shapes too began to turn ugly. Whatever the outcome, she'd meet it head on, as she always did. Deep down though, she wished, for once, things would just go her way.

CHAPTER SEVENTEEN

Running like she had never run before, Mira followed Stryker toward the cave where the rest of the group would be waiting.

Though sure she and Stryker had taken care of the humans that had been tracking her, she had not been able to rest. No, there would be no rest or calm in her mind until she saw with her own two eyes that her companions, and the wolves too, were alive and well.

Under a blanket of glorious twinkling stars, they bounded over rocks and weaved in and out of trees and bushes, following an unmarked trail only Stryker or a member of his pack would recognize. Wind rushing though her hair and the crisp clean air still fresh from the previous day's rain fortified her soul. Freedom was there, within her grasp. Just one more hurdle to overcome, and she and her human companions could live in peace.

Stryker zigged and zagged through the trees so fast that even Mira herself had a hard time following the trail. That gave her some peace. If the humans did ever decide to follow, they'd find it difficult to locate any real path. That, however, would not stop them from bulldozing their way through the ruined forest. Humans were tricky like that. Or perhaps, sloppy and brutish,

Mira thought. Either way, they would do whatever they had to in order to find what they wanted.

A light twinkled from a cave up ahead of them. It would be a bit of a scramble up some sharp rocks, but nothing too hard to reach on foot. The light, though, concerned her. Easy enough to spot from her vantage point on the ground, if someone had been following, they'd know exactly where the pack was hiding. Mira made a mental note to have them put out the light when she got up to them. Safety first. She didn't want anything to give away her position on the off chance more humans were around.

A dark-haired wolf acting as sentry met them just before they began their ascent to the cave. He shifted upon seeing Stryker and greeted his leader with a polite bow of his head.

Naked and unashamed, as all of the other wolves Mira had met, a tall figure stood before them without bothering to cover anything – something Mira felt she would never get used to. She hadn't intended to look, but it was so hard not to. She forced her eyes upwards and finally recognized the wolf as Terrance. He had to have caught her accidental peek. The smirk said it all. Mira tightened her jaw, setting her face as neutral as possible, and returned her focus to Stryker.

"Report," Stryker said, with all the command of his position as Alpha.

"We're all here and accounted for. I'm on second watch."

"What of our injured and the humans?"

"That human, Sarah" – There was no hint of spite, as Mira had expected; instead, Terrance actually sounded appreciative – "is quite accomplished with minor first aid. She's been keeping watch over the injured like a mother hen."

Mira stifled a laugh. The same woman who'd been squeamish when her husband was injured? She was taking care of wolves? Had she misread the quiet human?

"Are they well enough to travel?" Stryker asked.

"They're doing much better."

"Then let's get on the road. We don't need to waste more time. We can all head towards Caldera now."

Terrance's lips pursed tight. He didn't say it, but Mira got the impression that he was not sure of how to respond. Instead, he turned his uncertain gaze to Stryker.

Mira didn't need this pussyfooting. "We'll lose another day if we wait any longer. I get it, you all don't trust me. But the longer we leave ourselves out here in the open, the more opportunity we have of being found by the wrong sort. We'll get going now before any more humans can follow and sort out our issues from the safety of Sanctuary."

Terrance sucked in a worried breath but did not speak out. Instead he pleaded silently with his eyes at Stryker for a response.

Mira growled with frustration. "Stryker, tell them what we agreed, and let's get a move on."

Stryker crossed his arms, his expression thoughtful, as if trying to find the best way to explain things.

"Our orders were clear." Terrance's voice was weak. The younger wolf was in no position to challenge his elder, and the fear of reprisal was there in his eyes; though she couldn't tell if it was Stryker he feared, or the Council.

"I give the orders in this pack," Stryker finally spoke up. His tone, however, brooked no arguments. He held his head high, meeting the other wolf's eyes dead on. "Our situation has changed. We will have to present new evidence to the Council before a decision can be made. If you have a problem with this, speak now." He clenched his fists, a subtle motion meant to intimidate rather than spur on a fight. And it seemed Terrance got the message loud and clear. The lesser wolf bowed his head.

"Good." Stryker relaxed his fists. "I will tell the others of my decision. Terrance, I want you to go on ahead and alert the sentry that we'll all be arriving before morning." He turned to Mira. "I don't want to give them any surprises. They'll be more likely to listen if we're up front and open about things."

"Do what you feel is best." Mira wasn't sure she liked the idea of alerting the Council, but she'd come to trust Stryker.

"Terrance, be sure to let them know we were pursued by three tanks. I killed the last of them this afternoon."

Terrance nodded curtly at his Alpha, but the angry glare he sent her way was not lost on Mira. He'd been friendly enough the night before – what had changed? "Will that be all?" Terrance's voice had not lost the undertone of fear.

"Just go." Stryker commanded with a wave of his hand.

The scrappy looking wolf turned instantly into his other form and took off into the darkness.

"What's his problem with us now?" Mira asked.

"He doesn't want to die."

"Why would he?"

"The same threat that was delivered to you was given to us as well. We bring you all back as immortals or we die at the gate."

"They really need to work on their sales pitch." Mira, undeterred by the death threats, started her climb up to the cave.

"That's why I sent him ahead. He will not be held accountable, as the messenger. But I am sure he'll feel you are responsible if the rest of us are killed."

"Do you think that will actually happen?"

"Perhaps. It's entirely possible." He kept his tone neutral, though Mira was sure he had to be worrying about the outcome too. She was used to death threats, but doubted the Alpha got many in his time. Despite the seriousness of the situation, Stryker looked calm as ever.

"And you're willing to accept that?" Mira asked.

"The leaders have grown very cold these last few centuries. I would not assume anything where they are concerned. But, they should listen to reason – and reason will tell them that killing you is the wrong decision."

"You don't sound too convincing."

"That's because I am not convinced… that they will do the right thing here."

"Are they not good leaders?"

"Sure, but even good leaders are prone to making rash decisions when they feel the fate of their people is compromised."

"You think they will try to kill us all?"

Stryker shrugged as he passed her by, scrambling up the mountain in a rushed pace.

"Right," Mira sighed. "We're just going to hope for the best?"

"Mira, please… just have a little faith in me. Let's get the others ready and head out."

Trust and faith and positive thinking. These were dirty words to Mira, but if he could trust her, she had to give him the credit, too.

CHAPTER EIGHTEEN

T he troop moved swiftly upward toward the cave that would lead them to Caldera Grove.

Mira didn't quite know what to expect, but she prepared for the worst. Maybe they'd be shot on sight. Maybe Remy would have a choir of other sirens ready to sing them right off a cliff. The scenarios she imagined became more ridiculous the longer she thought about them. Death threats were something she was used to, but they weren't something to be taken lightly, and it was not only her life on the line. The whole pack as well as her human companions were on the chopping block.

Turning the humans against their will seemed more and more like the best choice when compared to the other option.

That's when she knew she her nerves were getting the better of her. Never before had she faced a battle with so much riding on it. It had always been her own life on the line, something she was okay with gambling. The same didn't apply when she actually cared about others and they were the ones at stake. She was determined that no matter the consequences, she'd fight to the death to keep her friends safe.

Closing in, the entrance to the cave became visible. Mira spotted Remy, the annoying singing siren. She recognized his short stature and ugly hat. That wasn't the only thing she noticed;

behind him, the Council was coming out to greet them. Not surprising.

Rather than slow down and prolong the inevitable, Mira sped up to meet them head on.

"What the hell is going on here?" Alec spoke before she'd even come to a stop. "You dare to defy my rule? You bring humans into our midst. We had a deal, vampire." His eyes turned an eerie gray as he locked on to her face.

She came to a sudden stop inches away from the Otherkin dwarf leader. Though short in stature, he was no less intimidating. Wearing ancient looking armor and carrying a large-handled axe, he was clearly ready for a fight. So too were the other members of the Council, all armored all carrying weapons. Others too were there, waiting behind the Council members. Soldiers perhaps. Mira had yet to be introduced, nor had she seen formal soldiers on her last visit. Their weapons, she noted, appeared new – they had a shine to them that went way beyond good care and maintenance. If she didn't know better, she'd have thought they'd never been used. Despite the disparity in in their numbers, Mira and her group might have a slight upper hand, being more adept at defending themselves. Not that she wanted to test that theory yet, but she would if it came to it.

Twitchy fingers near her belt, she stood ready to grab her dagger if necessary.

The others in her group came up short behind Mira. Wolves shifting into their human form took spots to her right, and the humans stood just to the left of her shoulder.

Still keeping his eyes locked on Mira, Alec waved a hand and two women, Otherkin she'd yet to be introduced to, seized hold of Curtis and Sarah.

Stryker grabbed Lucian and pulled him behind before anyone else could come near him.

Mira wasn't a wolf and would not let Alec's focused stare intimidate her. "What deal? You tried to force your will on me with that Otherkin skill of yours. That won't happen again, and you won't try it on my friends." She could hardly believe the word "friend" had left her lips, but when it did, she knew she meant it. They were more than just companions. They were her friends. People she could count on. They'd proven themselves. And human though they were, she was fond of them, and had already and would continue to look out for their welfare.

Remy, standing a few paces behind Alec and the rest of the Council, calmly hummed a tune. He smirked at Mira, taunting her with his eyes.

She refused to break eye contact with Alec, but shouted, "Don't listen to the siren. He's going to try to send you away."

"Damn you!" both Remy and Alec shouted.

"What's a siren?" Sarah whispered.

"Someone you don't need to trifle with." The woman holding her snarled.

"You let her go right now." Mira grabbed the dagger from her belt and crouched ready to strike at anyone who dared make a move at her.

"Release the humans for now," Natasha spoke calmly.

Surprised to see such civility from the dark-haired vampire, Mira relaxed her grip on the dagger. Maybe she had misread Natasha the first time she'd seen her in the Council chambers. Mira had pegged her for an ice queen with absolutely no care at all for the lives of humans. If Natasha wanted, she could snap the humans' necks in a heartbeat, and Mira would have no way to protect them all.

"I'm interested in hearing why you chose to break our rules." Natasha strolled over to Curtis, icy eyes inspecting the older gentleman's salt and pepper hair. She ran the back of her hand over his stubbly cheek, clearly in need of a shave. "What is it about you that makes this vampire so willing to ruin everything?" Her words had been spoken to Curtis but were clearly directed at Mira.

Nervous, but keeping a stiff upper lip about it, Curtis addressed the tall, slender vampire. "We're not all bad…us humans."

"Indeed." Natasha turned away, clearly unimpressed. "Mira, dear, there are reprisals for breaking the rules, no matter what the reason." Her tone may have been calm, but the threat was there. "Lesser vampires have died…"

"You deserve death." Alec, however, was not so subtle. "You've turned our wolves against us, you bring humans to our door, and from what I understand from our wolf patrol, more humans are on the way."

Mira caught sight of Terrance standing nervously toward the back of the cave. Eyes cast down to the ground, he noticeably avoided looking at his Alpha. Not a good sign at all.

Clenching her fist tighter again around her dagger, she glared back at the Otherkin dwarf. "The only thing you're mad at is the fact that I have not turned my friends against their will. All I wanted was to find refuge for me and my friends. We've been through so much, risked everything. Instead of welcome from my fellow people, I have been tricked, shunned, and lied to. You used your magical mumbo-jumbo to force me to betray my own friends so you could keep your segregated society closed to all but your own kind."

Niko had been watching the situation like the hawk he was, analyzing the posturing of all in attendance like a chess master ready to claim checkmate. "Our rules are set in place to protect our society and way of life. If you cannot abide by them, then you cannot be part of our society and claim sanctuary."

He may have looked meaner that the rest, but Niko appeared to have the calmest of heads among the angry mob. She directed her attention to him and relaxed the grip on her weapon. "Then leave us to our own devices. Put down your weapons, and let us walk away."

Still angry, Alec refused to back down. "That won't happen now. You know the path to our home. You will divulge our secrets."

So much for Niko's civility. Alec was determined to push for a battle. "You leave me with no choice then."

Mira's tone lowered to a dangerous level. "I've fought for my life for over thirty years; nothing will stop me from that now."

"Wait!" Stryker shouted. "This is insanity."

"You'll hold your tongue, wolf." Niko's tone sharpened. "The Council will decide what is best for the good of the community."

"You had a job to do, Stryker," Alec said. "You were to ensure she turned the humans. You could have prevented all of this. We hold you equally accountable."

Stryker joined Mira, standing shoulder to shoulder with her. "Our situation has changed. The enemy is at our gate."

"Yes, we can plainly see this." Natasha almost appeared as if she wanted to laugh at his obviousness.

"Wrong enemy." Deadly serious, Stryker's tone deepened to a rumbling growl.

"Respect, wolf." Niko warned.

"I've patrolled this area for decades. It used to be that the humans would never come across the badlands. They didn't have the technology or were too afraid. Whatever the reason, they left our borders alone. Now in three days' time, we have seen tanks and soldiers, and have lost members of our pack due to human encroachment."

"Because of them." Alec threw an accusatory finger at Mira.

She'd love to bite that thing off, but didn't want to interrupt Stryker. He more than made up for her lack of diplomacy.

Stryker calmed the anger in his voice. "Today, tomorrow, Mira, or someone else, the reason is irrelevant. The humans will eventually come. That fact cannot be disputed."

"But they are coming now, as a result of this woman," Alec responded.

"Forget this woman and forget these humans for now. We have a bigger battle to worry about. Humans from the Iron Gate city will come back. They'll not stop now that they've made it this far. Can't we set aside our disagreement until after we solve our problems? Mira is an accomplished fighter; she'd be good on our side." Stryker pulled Lucian forward. "This human here. He's a former Elite; he knows things about their society. He can help us find their weaknesses."

Not one to show his intimidation, Lucian, who'd calmly stood by, finally spoke. "Yes. I would be happy to offer you any help I can."

"Silence, human. You have no say here." Alec lowered his axe in an attempt to intimidate.

Mira caught sight of Lucian's nostrils flaring angrily, but being the better man about it, he held his tongue. His eyes met hers, and she understood he was and deferring to her rather than spitefully responding. Smart man. She, however, was not so diplomatic.

"You'll want to be a little nicer to my friends," she snarled.

The look on Lucian's face at the sound of the word "friend" was priceless. Clearly, he was just as shocked as she was to hear the word out loud.

"Everyone needs to calm down. Nothing good will come of a fight." Stryker addressed the angry dwarf. "You know as well as I that Mira's no stranger to fighting for her life. When was the last time you used that axe in battle?"

The dwarf's face turned a deep shade of angry red. He mashed his teeth together, and Mira could swear she heard a rumbling coming from Alec's throat. He looked as if he was about to blow his top.

Niko, remaining the calmest of the bunch, placed a hand on Alec's shoulder. "Easy, brother. The wolf, though disrespectful, has a point."

Despite suddenly not caring whether or not she was allowed in Sanctuary, Mira liked the sound of Stryker's plan. Working together using all of their skills would be best. They could meet the humans head on and maybe even drive them back to the city. She'd be able to keep her promise to George, too. "I have friends on the inside of the Iron Gate prison as well – warriors, like me. If you all drop the death threats, we can word towards some kind of arrangement. Maybe we find a way to free them. Imagine what kind of an army you would have with hard-core trained fighters on your side."

Alec should have appreciated that plan, but being the hotheaded dwarf, he scoffed at the idea. "We have our own warriors."

Now it was Mira's turn to laugh. She glanced around the cave. New weapons, shiny armor that had hardly a scuff mark? None of these soldiers here were trained fighters. She wondered if a demonstration was in order, but thought better of it. Alec was already too close to blowing up. She's just have to attack him with words until she provoked a physical reaction. "No offense. No, wait… actually I do mean to offend you." She cast a sidelong glance at the others with their bright, shiny, unused weapons. "I could mop the floor with what I see of your warriors."

Stryker cast a wary glance at her.

Mira shrugged. "Hey, he wants to boast, but when it comes down to it, you want the real deal on your side... unless you just want to lose. And from what I see, the stakes couldn't be any higher. Lucian can attest to the horrors the human race is capable of. And they've got plenty of weapons to back themselves up."

The Council members all exchanged guarded glances. Tension ran thick as the silent moments dragged on. No one dared to make a move, but everyone was wound tighter than a spring ready to be sprung. Just one word from either side and an all-out war would be started.

Finally, Alec let out a loud defeated sigh and lowered his weapon. "We will discuss your proposal in Council." He took a few slow steps backwards, not turning his back to the group. "You all, Stryker included, will stay here until a decision is made." He disappeared into the hidden entrance of the rock.

The rest of the Council followed behind Alec; they, however, did not worry about turning their backs on Mira or her human friends.

"Thanks for your defense." Mira nodded to Stryker. "You took a big risk, going up against your leaders."

Worry clouded his warm amber eyes. Stryker sat down on the ground and began his ritual of drawing in the dirt. "I am the leader of my pack. And I decide what is best for them. You are good people. Your plight is the same as all of our kind, only you are much closer to the actual danger. Our people have grown soft, comfortable in their security. What I said was truth. They might have taken it as disrespect because it was not what they wanted to hear, but it needed to be said. Whether it was you or someone else down the line who brings the humans to our door, it will happen eventually. We can't take on the humans as we are now."

Lucian crouched down next to Stryker. The simplicity of watching someone doodle in the sand had caught his interest as it had Mira's days before.

"Do you mean for us to go up against all eight colonies?" Lucian asked.

"We never wanted to be part of a war," Curtis finally spoke, his voice warbling with fear. "We've been through so much in these last few days. More than we had ever expected."

Lucian stood and squeezed Curtis's shoulder. "You've gone above and beyond, my friend."

"I'm not saying I won't do what's required of me, but my poor Sarah…"

"I'm fine, love," Sara pulled her husband into a tight hug. "As long as we're together, I can withstand anything."

The skinny woman looked as if she'd blow away in a strong breeze. No. Mira couldn't involve her in a fight.

"You both have done enough. I don't want you to worry. Whatever happens, I'll protect you. Your job is done."

The other wolves milled about the cave anxiously. Remy kept his distance, but shot furtive glances back at Mira. The threat from the council may have been taken away for the moment, but there was still a lot of animosity in the air. Terrance, though part of Stryker's pack, still kept to himself alone along the back wall.

"Don't you all see how pointless this is?" Mira directed her question to everyone keeping their distance in the cave. "We could all be enjoying this beautiful starry sky and fresh air, but because of your stupid prejudices, you're standing in there waiting for the word to fight and have me kill you. I don't want to kill you either. I want to be your… frien… I want to get to know you all better. To live with you in peace."

Remy pulled his ugly hat off his head. He bit his lip and nodded. "You got a point." He walked forward and held out his hand. "Truce."

She took the offered hand. "Was that so hard?"

"Yes," Remy said with a smirk.

"Now we just need to get the rest of the Council to let go of that stupid ignorance."

"Hey, now…"

"I'm not saying you're stupid… just your actions."

Stryker looked up from his drawing. "You don't erase centuries of hatred in minutes."

"Never said I wanted to erase it. But if you don't give people a chance…"

Lucian stood and reaching out a hand, walked over to Mira. Uncertain of what he was doing, she hesitated when he took her hand and stroked it. "I'm so very glad you took a chance on me, Mira. Thanks for not killing me in that hallway."

Best decision of her life. Mira met Lucian's mossy eyes with a smile. He'd been the first human to show her kindness. And that small spark gave her faith that humanity was not all a lost cause. "You wouldn't have made a good meal anyway." Of course she didn't want to let on that she had a soft spot for the handsome human.

"Always the attitude. Do you ever let your guard down?" Lucian looked as if he was hiding his hurt feelings, but his tone remained light.

"You know how I feel about that."

Stryker cleared his throat. "Back to the matter at hand. The Iron Gate humans need to be taught a lesson. I'm not saying we have to fight every last one of them, but we need to hit them hard and make it known that we are a force to be reckoned with. If nothing else, it will teach them not to come after us again."

Lucian released Mira's hand. "If I may, we can hit them hard, but as long as the Magistrate is in power there will be no end to the battle. You will need to kill him."

Though she'd felt uncomfortable holding it, she found she missed the warmth of Lucian's hand. "Make an example of him, though. Put his crimes on display. You want the humans to stop coming after our kind, but you also want them to see us for the people we are… not savages, not bloodthirsty. They need to see that we're capable of thoughts, feelings, and most of all, that we have a conscience. That's the biggest problem with the human population at this time. They do not think us… well, vampires, that is, capable of rational thought. We're nothing more than beasts to them. Which is why they don't care when we're slaughtered."

"Well, before we can do anything to the humans, we must secure the support of the Council." Stryker's voice lacked enthusiasm. "I'm not confident that we'll get that."

"They may not have a choice," Mira said. "As you clearly pointed out, the battle is at their door already, thanks to us."

"Yes, but they suffer from a bit of the same arrogance as your humans do. It's been centuries since they've had to face any opposition. They feel comfortable in their superiority and strength. They've never been tested."

"They can be superior all the way to the grave," Mira scoffed.

"I'm not arguing with you, I'm merely pointing out where their thoughts will be," Stryker said.

"Then if they don't agree, we'll have to make them see reason." Mira punched her hand.

"Knock some sense into them?" Stryker asked.

"Was that you making a joke, wolfman? I like it." Mira laughed. "But yeah, to be blunt, if they need to see where their weakness lies, I'll be more than happy to show them."

"That won't be necessary." Alec had returned with the rest of the Council, sounding calmer than he had earlier. "Your presence here has caused a great disturbance in our way of life. But, though we are loath to endure it, we must. If not now, some other time in the future this would have happened. Stryker is right: We do need to meet the threat of the humans' encroachment head on. And, it has been pointed out we also need to help our imprisoned brothers in need."

"So then you'll fight with us?" Mira asked.

"We will fight the battles we can win. As you have so clearly pointed out, we are not as strong as we should be. We need reinforcements."

That raised Mira's eyebrow.

"You will provide them."

"Oh?" she asked.

"We'll make you a new deal. I want you to take a team back to the human city. You spoke of the other vampires who would fight alongside of us. Free them and bring them with you. If you can do this, we'll combine our forces and create an army capable of taking on the humans."

There were far too many ifs in that sentence, but at least they were heading in the right direction with their so-called deal.

"Fine. But while this is happening, what of my friends?" Mira's question was directed at Alec, but her eyes fell on Curtis and Sarah, weary and tired, sitting together on the ground. "I need to be assured of their comfort and safety."

Alec's jaw tightened. He took a breath and calmed himself before speaking. "As for the humans, they'll be allowed within our sanctuary, as our… guests." He cringed as he said the word. It was apparently taking all his control to keep his voice expressionless. "But, they cannot leave under any circumstances until the battle is won."

By the sound of it, she wasn't sure she could trust his word. "I'll need your assurance that they'll be comfortable and safe – something more than just your word."

Alec sneered. His eyes shot daggers at Mira. "My word should be more than adequate for you, vampire."

"Your word means nothing to me. You have not earned my trust."

"I don't have to earn it. I am the leader of the…"

Natasha spoke up. "I give you my blood oath as one of your own. This oath is witnessed by all present. The humans, Sarah, Curtis, and Lucian will remain here, comfortable and safe."

"And remain human?" Mira asked.

"Yes," Natasha answered. "They will remain as they are, so long as it is their wish to do so."

"No compulsion." Mira directed her comment at Alec, knowing full well he'd probably planned to trick them while she was otherwise occupied.

Alec's sneer faded. "No tricks. No games. We will not alter them in any way. Do we have a deal, vampire?"

"Almost. What are the terms of this deal should I not return?"

Natasha spoke up before Alec had the chance to answer. "Your sacrifice will be honored, Mira, and your friends will live out their life in peace."

Mira took a slow deep breath. She looked out of the cave, up at the stars. The glorious stars that she'd waited more than thirty years to see.

This new "deal" was anything but. To go back to New Haven, back behind the Iron Gate and not only live to tell the tale but also free a prison full of vampires in the center of the city? It was a suicide mission. One she was sure she'd never make it back from. But her friends would be safe. That was what mattered now. They'd risked their lives for her; now it was her turn. It was the right thing. The honorable thing to do.

With a heavy sigh, Mira turned back to the council members, meeting each of them in the eyes in turn. "Deal."

REVOLUTION

Chronicles of the Uprising: 3
Sample
Chapter 1

Silvery moonlight bled through the sheer curtains above Mira's head. Cradled in the warmth of the pillowy mattress, Mira could have stayed in bed for all eternity. She could hardly remember a time when she'd been so comfortable. Thirty years in a dirty cell had made her forget the simple comforts of a warm bed and soft clothes. The breeze drifted in, picking up the curtains and sending them lazily dancing. She reached up, letting them tickle her fingertips, and noticed something she'd ever seen before. Well, at least something she hadn't seen in a very long time. Her hands were clean. Truly clean... and soft. No caked-on blood and grime, or gunk embedded into her nail beds. They even smelled of lemongrass and sandalwood, and were smoother than she'd ever known, thanks to the oils and lotions Stryker had provided her. This was how things were supposed to be. Life was not supposed to be dirty and ugly. Life was meant to be lived, and small comforts like this enjoyed, not ended by the swift stroke of her sword at the order of her masters. Though she missed the comfortable weight of her weapon, she'd gladly give it up if it meant never having to fight again.

She sighed contentedly and let the squishy mattress hug every inch of her body. This was heaven.

If she could somehow stop time, make the moment last forever, she would. Not being a very devout vampire, Mira still silently prayed – begged really – to the gods for more of this blissful peace. Hope kept the dream alive, but Mira knew the truth. This was only a brief peaceful interlude, one she so desperately needed, but it would be short-lived.

Mira was a warrior. Fighting was her life, try as she might to deny it, and the looming dread of what was to come weighed heavily on her heart.

She should have been up and moving, sunset having long since passed, but she couldn't tear her eyes away from the window. So many evenings lost. So many missed opportunities to take in the breathtaking majesty of the starlit sky. Thirty years of imprisonment deep underground had robbed her of everything she'd once taken for granted, and now that she was finally able to see and appreciate the twinkling stars, Mira wasn't wasting one second of it.

In less than forty-eight hours, she'd be back on the road to almost certain death.

She pulled a soft knit blanket up to her shoulders to ward off the slight chill in the air.

Everything comes with a price. Caldera Grove. Beautiful, mystical, and earthy, it promised that longed-for freedom to Mira, and a life free of prejudice. But that did not extend to the humans who'd accompanied her. Lucian, Sarah, and Curtis's fate depended on Mira. She'd already paid dearly in the struggle for her own freedom, but it had not been enough to ensure her friends' safety. The price promised to cost her more than she would be able to pay… a trip back to New Haven, behind the Iron Gate.

Hardened warrior as she was, thinking of returning to that dreadful place made her cringe. Silver-coated bars. UV torches. The lightbox. Thirty years spent trying to escape from within those walls. Enduring unbearable tortures and being forced to kill for the entertainment of her masters.

Anger turned to bile in the back of her throat, threatening to sour the peaceful moment she'd been enjoying.

It was best not to think of such things. Live in the moment. Enjoy the comfort. Savor the delectably squishy mattress at her back, and the chilly breeze blowing in. These luxuries deserved to be cherished.

"Mira, are you up?" Lucian's voice, muffled slightly, penetrated the thick wooden door of the room she was using for sleep. "We're scheduled to meet with the Council."

The root of her latest set of problems. The Otherkin Council. Mira grumbled, "Bunch of pompous asses. Self-absorbed and out of touch..." Other choice descriptions came to mind, but name-calling wasn't going to change the fact that she owed them a debt that had to be paid. And she had to at least make the effort to play nicely until she left the walls of Caldera Grove. She was just as much on their good side as they were hers. But, it was by their good graces she and the humans had been allowed within the boundaries of Caldera Grove, and she had to cooperate, much as it annoyed her to do so.

Lucian must not have heard her grumbling. He knocked on the door and waited a moment before saying, "Mira? Can I come in?"

She wanted to say no. His very presence reminded her of the duty she must perform, and all she wanted to do at that moment was forget her troubles. Heaving a heavy sigh, Mira reluctantly tossed aside her blanket and stood. "Yeah, get in here!"

Lucian pushed the door open but did not step inside. "Making yourself at home, I see." His mossy eyes spoke more than words about his discomfort and deep-rooted anger.

"Shouldn't I be as comfortable as possible while I can?" Damn his silent judgment of her. She deserved a little rest and recuperation after all she'd been through. "It's not often I get to enjoy such luxury."

She could see the words forming, but Lucian did not speak them. Nothing about this place was luxurious to him, nor was he happy with their situation.

"Have you been mistreated?" she asked, wondering if she'd missed something beyond their hosts' prejudice.

"Quite the contrary." Lucian folded his arms and leaned against the doorframe. His posture might have looked relaxed, but she saw past the ruse to the Elite within him, rising to the surface. The pampered prince throwing a temper tantrum, but desperately trying to hide it. "Stryker's pack has been quite congenial. But we're quarantined here. Only allowed to leave with your escort. I'd have loved to explore the city."

"You will in time." Mira tried to hold back the smirk. Thirty years she'd been imprisoned in a tiny cell, and he was daring to complain to her about having to stay inside the wolf-pack's large den all day? In some ways, though she dare not admit it out loud, she felt a little vindication seeing Lucian's discomfort. After all, he had enjoyed his Elite status and all that entailed while she'd spent all those years as a gladiator.

"Yes, of course. I'll be able to explore after the suicide mission." Sarcasm made him sound petulant, but she decided best not to call him out on it yet. "Assuming, that is, I make it back in one piece. Speaking of that, we should head to our meeting about our impending death. The Council is waiting."

"Don't sound so positive, Lucian. People will think we've swapped bodies."

His eyes narrowed slightly, forming tiny creases at the corners. "Are you not bothered by the fact we are going to die?"

Mira shook her head. Death threats had been her way of life for so long they'd become white noise. Of course she was not ready to die, but there was no point in acknowledging those fears. "Everyone dies eventually. Enjoy the ride and make the trip worthwhile."

"Spoken like someone ready to die." His tone fell flat, as If he'd already accepted defeat and the inevitable.

As much as she owed him her allegiance, his mood swings were testing the limits of her patience. "I can see you're stressed, so I'll forgive the temper tantrum this time... Suck it up, Elite."

Her use of that word had the intended effect, rendering Lucian speechless. Jaw hanging wide, he looked positively stunned. Behind his eyes she saw a multitude of emotions fighting to surface. She stared him down, daring him to say something else stupid and give her a reason to shut him up. He was better than this. She knew it. This moodiness had to stop, one way or another.

After the moment had passed, and he appeared to have calmed, Mira spoke again. "Will Sarah and Curtis be joining us?"

"They're required to attend." Though much calmer now, contempt still tainted his voice. "Escorted guard and all."

"You're going to have to drop the attitude. The tables have turned. You're no Elite here. You are nothing to them... until you show them your worth."

Lucian let out a sigh. His shoulders slumped. "You're right. I'm being an arrogant idiot about all of this."

"Remember, those are your words, not mine." Though she whole-heartedly agreed with them.

"These last few days have been so trying."

Mira closed the gap between them. Her first thought was to reach out and comfort him, but stopped herself. Touching was what other people did, hugging and hand holding. She could try to emulate it, give the pouting human what he wanted. But unnecessary touching felt odd and mechanical. Physical contact wasn't what he needed anyway. A swift kick in the ego would do. "I'm trying my best not to laugh now."

Her snarky comment earned a much more acceptable impish smile from the human. "Laughing at my misfortune; how very magnanimous of you." Lucian crossed his arms, making him look even more the pouting child.

"Not sure what that word means, but sure. I've been tortured and damn near killed. Risked my life and put my neck on the line for you… and you're grumpy."

"And pouting like a little child. Yes. I hear you loud and clear. I'll shut up now."

"Finally." She winked. "We're on the same page."

"I'm just not used to this. Not that it should be an excuse, I know. I'll suck it up, as you said, and try harder to be accepting of their … hospitability."

"I wouldn't go as far as calling them hospitable just yet. They're only harboring you until the outcome of the suicide mission."

Finally, his mood truly lifted, and Lucian even let slip a laugh. "I love how blunt you are, Mira."

"Pussy-footing doesn't get you anywhere. And neither does procrastination. Let's get moving." She grabbed a light shawl from a hanger by the door and threw it over her shoulders. The air in Caldera was chillier than she was used to, and though she enjoyed it, Mira was finding it left her cold to the bones after only a short while. Blame slow vampire circulation for that, but at least there were warm clothes to compensate.

The wolves' den was surprisingly quiet at this early hour of the night. Their room was one of many off the great circular shaped living space. Even to her enhanced hearing, there were hardly any sounds of life in the building. Two figures, human by the smell of them, were lounging by the fire, but aside from that, the place was empty. Odd, she thought. Mira would have expected to see at least some of the pack milling about in the great room. They had, after all, been told they had to have an escort anywhere they went. Why leave them alone, then? Questions for another time.

Mira headed for the door, expecting a guard to be placed there, but again found nothing. Not that they could go far on their own; Caldera was far from a huge city, and they were obviously newcomers. On orders to stay put until an escort came for them, any misstep would certainly be reported. *Oh, well.* She'd deal with the repercussions if any arose; they were meant to go visit the Council anyway. She opened the door, intending to walk there herself, when Stryker rounded the corner at the end of the street. He spotted her and waved.

As escorts went, he was certainly preferable. She knew he was on her side of things. And not too bad in a fight, either. She waved back and waited for him to make it to the door.

Fresh from a run, he had the scent of sweat on his skin, but Mira secretly felt a pang of disappointment that he was clothed instead of in his usual natural state. Shifters did not seem to mind nudity, and neither did Mira. A well-toned body was always a sight to appreciate.

"Drooling again, Mira?" Stryker flashed her a toothy grin as he brushed past her in the doorway. She purposely stood her ground so they would touch and she could get a deeper breath of his manly scent before it was gone.

Lucian crossed his arms, setting his mouth into a hard line. Not sure if his aggressive stare was directed at Mira or Stryker, she shrugged it off and licked her fangs. "Hungry, actually."

"Wild for more wolf, eh?" Stryker's amber eyes sparkled at her.

That got a rise out of Lucian. The air of Elite decorum fell as he practically snarled, "You fed from him?"

"Yeah, why?" Confused by his appalled tone, Mira stepped back from both men.

Eyes cast down to the ground with uncharacteristic abashment, Lucian quietly mumbled, "Nothing. I forget your nature sometimes."

There was more behind his words, but Mira had neither the time nor the desire to drag it out of him. She was a vampire. She was free. She could feed on whomever she pleased.

Unfazed by either her comments or Lucian's grimacing face, Stryker walked passed Mira into the house. "Let me change, and I'll escort you to the meeting. You can stop by the clinic if you need to, Mira. There should be donors available."

"I can wait until we've finished our meeting. As I understand it, we've inconvenienced the Council enough."

"Don't pretend you care," Stryker laughed. He disappeared behind a door. Mira could hear him moving about in the room.

Lucian stood awkwardly silent for a few moments before he finally spoke. "I'll go speak with Sarah and Curtis until we are ready to leave." He turned away from Mira and walked toward another set of doors off the circular main room.

"We're here." Curtis lifted a hand and waved at his leader. He and his wife sat snuggled up together in a large cushioned seat near the fire. "Just waiting on you, sir."

Lucian walked passed, brushing Mira's shoulder roughly with his own as he headed toward the fire. Passive aggressive was not becoming on him, though she read the message loud and clear: he was disappointed with her, but for what reason, she couldn't fathom. Humans were so touchy about things at times.

Stryker reemerged from his room dressed in linen pants and a long tunic belted at the waist, similar to what she'd been outfitted in when she was a gladiator. It struck her as odd to see someone from this place dressed like a slave. "Do you think I'll pass for one of your prisoners?"

The question was directed at Lucian, but Stryker looked almost excitedly at Mira.

She shrugged, trying not to let the anguish she felt remembering her time in the prison rise to the surface. "Looks too clean."

"We'll dirty it up on the way, then." Stryker closed the gap between himself and Mira. "If we can utilize the element of surprise…"

"I see where you're going with this, but slaves are imprisoned when they are not fighting. You'd never find one roaming the halls, and certainly not without guard."

"Details I've considered. I have the uniforms from the soldiers we felled on our journey."

His attention to detail impressed Mira. A warrior with a sharp mind too. No wonder he was an Alpha. She was glad she had him on her side. He had already proved to be so helpful and would continue to be so. "You surprise me, wolf."

"I'll take that as a compliment, vampire." He winked and flashed her a devilish grin. She loved their little jabs, the playful to and fro between them. Stryker was so easy to get along with.

"I'll take you all now to the Council chambers." Stryker waved his hand directing everyone out of the house.

REVOLUTION

Chronicles of the Uprising: 3
Sample
Chapter 2

They walked along the moonlit roads toward the center of Caldera, Stryker and Mira taking the lead with the humans close behind. Though she'd seen it all before on her previous visit, Mira couldn't help but slow her pace so she could properly take in the sights and smells of this paradise for the supernatural. Only a short while ago, this place had been all but myth to her, and now she was *this close* to calling it her home.

Knowing it was folly, she dared to dream that one day it just might be the place she called home. Suicide mission or not.

Middle of the night as it was, the city was alive and vital. Vampires, shifters, and Otherkin alike were busy with the hustle and bustle of their nightly activities. Small shop owners with their doors wide open to the night air waved and smiled, inviting Mira's small group inside for a peek at their wares. Although she was tempted, Mira didn't stray from her path. But she did promise herself plenty of time for exploration when they came back victorious. She smiled and waved back at those who were courteous to her. Being a prisoner had not stripped her of manners, though some might have thought that was the case.

Not all passersby looked on Mira's group with friendly eyes, however. She noticed more than one wayward glance or suspicious glare from residents of the city. She expected as much for her companions – humans, after all – but not to her from her own kind. Their visible anger made Mira feel ill at ease. The Council was already breathing down her throat; she had not considered having to win over the city inhabitants too. The hope of peace, the small spark she'd been holding onto so fiercely, suddenly dimmed.

"They know you brought the humans," Stryker answered her unasked question, thankfully without a hint of anger or condescension in his voice. "You'd be hard-pressed to find any popularity right now."

Mira shrugged, hoping to hide the worry she felt rising to the surface. "I don't need popularity, just acceptance." In truth, she needed both. Not necessarily popularity in the traditional sense, but kinship, companionship – people like her who valued her. Being a slave for so long and having her only value be the amount of wins she'd racked up had skewed her sense of self-worth. Deep down she longed for someone to like her for something beyond her ability to rip a throat out.

"Acceptance you can have easily enough. You're one of us. But them…" Stryker cocked his head sideways and glanced back at the human trio following behind. "They'll probably never find acceptance here as long as they remain human."

Still pushing for her to turn them, even after she'd put her foot down. Would he ever stop? "I still think that's petty. Just for the record."

Now it was Stryker's turn to shrug, but he wasn't doing it to hide anything, Mira knew he didn't care one way or the other. "It is what it is. We just have to deal with it."

"Maybe not. We're going on a suicide mission, remember?"

"Always the optimist, aren't we?"

"Realist. How many times do I have to say it?"

"Well, realistically, we do stand a chance. We just need a good plan to get in and get your vampires released. I'm quite certain they can take care of the nitty gritty parts of continuing their freedom."

"Delicately put," Mira snickered. *Why must everyone pussyfoot around the topic of drinking blood?*

"I do try. Maybe you should too." His smile went far beyond playful, but the message was as serious as the grave.

"Is that your nice way of telling me to shut up and let others do the talking?" Her mouth had always been a problem. And though she hated to be reminded of that fact, she knew there was truth there. She often let it run wild, and this was not the time for it. At least Stryker was trying to tell her nicely; that was more courtesy than she'd been given in more years than she could count.

"No. Don't shut up. Your input is valid… just maybe try not to piss anyone off with it. Filter your words. We're trying to be on the same team here."

"You and my friends back there are on the same team. But… the Council… I have my doubts."

"They have the best interests of our people at heart, as hard as that may be to believe from your standpoint… And, yes, when I say *our* people, I am including you."

"Well, when I say my people, I am talking about my fri…" The word was right there on the tip of her tongue, and still she had trouble saying it. "Friends." She hadn't really had friends in so long. But that was what they were.

"And I mean to include them too. But for the Council's sake, filter… okay?"

Mira sighed. He was right. "I'll be as nice as I can be."

The quiet serenity of Caldera Grove made an impression on more than just Mira. She caught the same sparkle in Lucian's moss-green eyes that she'd had on her first visit. This city was unlike anything she'd seen before. Even in her early human days on the farm, she'd never experienced such oneness with nature, and no doubt Lucian, Curtis, and Sarah never had either. Raised in New Haven's concrete jungle, the lush green nature-loving city contrasted so sharply it bordered on unbelievable. Patchwork carpets of lush green grass surrounded the buildings, creating a gentle buffer between each and the road they walked on. Trees sprang up unobstructed, some even growing through the houses near which they had taken root. Branches jutted out oddly from walls with special holes in them to give the tree room to grow over time. This closeness with nature had perplexed and intrigued Mira the first time she'd seen it. Now, seeing it through the eyes of her companions seared into her mind how utterly different these two races had become. That planted tiny seeds of doubt in her mind. *What if the humans and the Otherkin could not get along? What if their differences were insurmountable?* She was preparing to risk life and limb going back to the human city, but her human friends here could be in peril.

Doubt and worry had been foreign concepts to Mira in the past. And that was how she liked it. These new protective feelings caused a small uncomfortable pang in her chest.

She'd rather be fighting than constantly concerned for the wellbeing of others. Tedious and troublesome worries dampened her sharp edge, and she needed to be on her game when they headed back to New Haven.

"How long have you all been here?" Lucian's amazement could not be contained.

"Since just after the Iron Gates were built." Stryker's tone did not betray any emotion. Even if it had, Mira doubted Lucian was truly listening. He had wandered over to a large garden and was admiring the flowers still open and reaching up to the moonlight. Childlike in innocence, he almost squealed in delight as he bent down to touch the soft petals. Moonlight might have muted the pinks, yellows, and purples, but that did not seem to dampen his appreciation of them. Lucian plucked a large five-petal white and yellow flower.

Before he could stand and turn with his new treasure, Stryker was on him. "What the hell do you think you're doing?"

Lucian wasn't the only one confused by the wolf's sudden aggression. "Sorry. I just…" His eyes frantically searched for a safe place to land and when they met Mira's, Lucian scrambled over to her. "A flower for the lady."

All the highborn Elite rose right to the surface, washing away the awkwardness he'd shone only moments prior. He held the flower to Mira. "Please… for you."

Now she was truly confused. Did she look like the kind of girl you gave a flower to? What was he playing at?

Silent moments passed with him holding the flower and Mira standing frozen in her spot looking utterly confused, not wanting to take it.

Stryker took a deep loud breath. "We do not remove the flowers from their place, so that all may enjoy their beauty."

"My apologies." Lucian addressed Stryker, but his gaze was fixed on Mira.

"I don't want the flower," Mira finally said, relieved to have a legitimate reason to reject the offered gift. "Especially if it will piss off our hosts."

Lucian put the small flower through the button hole of his shirt. "We come from different cultures. Giving a flower is…"

Stryker cut him off. "I don't care about your ways. We are not in your city. What grows in the ground has its own purpose.

Flowers are beautiful to look at and provide pollen for the bees –
who in turn provide us with honey as well as continual pollina-
tion. It is a cycle that should not be broken just for the sake of
turning a pretty woman's eye."

Testosterone and the unchecked aggression between the two
men were beginning to get on Mira's nerves.

"Perhaps we can just move on." Sarah's small voice seemed
to do the trick. Both men snapped to attention. Mira was never
more thankful for the interruption she provided.

Stryker's temper subsided. He turned to the older human
woman, his voice much calmer. "Yeah. Keep heading down this
road. We're nearly there."

Lucian moved quickly to rejoin his two human friends, and
Stryker matched pace with Mira.

"Didn't you just tell me to be nice, not five minutes ago?"
Mira asked.

"Yes… to the Council. Your friends are not that important."

"Careful, wolf. They are important to me."

Unfazed by her warning tone, Stryker shrugged. "No matter.
They will have to learn out ways. Play by our rules, if they plan to
co-exist here."

She couldn't argue that fact. This place went beyond culture
shock… in a good way, and would take a lot of getting used to.
"They will. Give them time. What is your problem with Lucian,
anyway?"

"He's human."

She turned a knowing eye on him. "It goes beyond his humanity. You only prickle like this when he's around me."

"He has feelings for you."

"So?" She'd thought the same thing, but that didn't matter
much to her. She'd never dared to open her heart again. Not

since Theo's death all those years ago. Emotions were messy and more painful than any lightbox the humans could concoct.

"He's human."

"You've said that."

"He has no business having feelings for an Otherkin."

"Really?" Not that she was putting herself on the market, but she didn't much like the wolf's implication that Lucian's species took him out of the running. The fact that Stryker claimed her to be of his kind, though, really threw her off guard. She'd never really felt she *belonged* anywhere before. "Is that all?"

Stryker hesitated. "Yes."

Mira had to hold back her snickering. She rather enjoyed seeing the wolfman trying hide whatever it was he was feeling.

"Well. Feelings are pretty useless things anyways. And besides that, I'm not spoken for, so whoever wants to have feelings can have them. I'm certainly not going to stop them."

If an Alpha could look wounded, Stryker was making a good attempt. Either way, it wasn't a good look for him. Maybe she'd struck a nerve with him. He couldn't really harbor feelings for her. He'd only just met her. She scoffed silently. *Feelings are such messy things.*

The hurt extended to Stryker's tone. "If feelings are so useless, then why didn't you take the flower he offered you?"

Mira shrugged, more to herself than in response to his question. Why hadn't she taken it? Lucian looked terribly awkward holding it. She knew he'd been offering it as a kindness, but somehow, doing it in front of Stryker felt so wrong. "What am I going to do with a flower? Hold it while it dies?"

Stryker smiled and tousled her black hair playfully. "You could place it in your hair."

She couldn't contain her laughter. "You're kidding, right? What kind of girl do you think I am? Next you're going to tell me I should wear a dress." *That'll be the day.*

"I can see why you're not accustomed to people having feelings for or around you. You lack any girlish qualities."

"Is that supposed to insult me?"

"Did it?"

"You'll have to try harder than that."

"Only if you give me plenty more opportunities to do that."

Now who was the one playing games with feelings? That odd awkward sensation came back, doubly so when she spotted Lucian's concerned expression. He'd stopped short and stood with his arms crossed, watching like a man ready to go to war.

"Something wrong?" Mira asked, but she had the sneaking suspicion she knew the answer.

"Just concerned… wondering how we should go about things… with regard to the meeting." All diplomat, but Lucian's tone spoke volumes of what he really wanted to say. He was just as annoyed with her talking to Stryker as the wolf had been with Lucian's interactions with her.

"You'll do best to let me and Mira handle things." Diplomacy had left Stryker, and his response dripped with condescension. "Speak when spoken to. Be brief and respectful."

Lucian's lips pursed tight. His nostrils flared with each breath, but he held his tongue.

The testosterone was thick enough to choke her, and she needed to snap these two idiots out of it. "Lucian's input is invaluable," Mira said. "He is, after all, an Elite of the city. That brings with it some important inside information. He will speak when he has need to. And so will our friends." She motioned toward Curtis and Sarah.

Hints of apprehension flashed in their eyes. Sarah sighed. "We don't want to cause any trouble." She clung tightly to her husband. "We're just glad for the chance to have a home and will do whatever is needed of us."

"And that is exactly what the Council needs to see. Humans are not the enemy. They can co-exist." Mira was never more proud to have Sarah along. They might have gotten off to a rocky start, but she'd proven many times over that she was an asset. "Now, we just need to make sure you and Lucian set that example too." She glared at Stryker.

He met her eyes, staring back with all the power of his Alpha status behind him. "I will do my part. You make sure to be polite – all of you – and we will get through this."

"Oh… I'll kill them with kindness."

That snapped the Alpha from his dominance stare and in an instant, the aggression faded into genuine amusement. "I'd like to see you try."

OTHER TITLES BY KATIE SALIDAS

The Immortalis Series:

Becoming a vampire is easy. Living with the condition... that's the hard part. Join Alyssa as she stumbles through the world of the "Unnatural."

Book 1: Immortalis Carpe Noctem - Newbie vampire Alyssa never asked for this life, but now it's all she has. Rescued from death by Lysander, the aloof and sexy leader of the Peregrinus vampire clan, she's barely cut her teeth before she becomes a target. Kallisto, an ancient and vindictive vampire queen – and Lysander's old mate - wants nothing less than final death for her former lover and his new toy. She's not above letting the Acta Sanctorum, and its greatest vampire hunter, Santino, know exactly where the clan can be found.With no time to mourn her old life, Alyssa's survival depends on her new family. She will have to stand alongside Lysander and fight against two enemies who will stop at nothing to destroy them.

Book 2: Hunters & Prey - Rule number one: humans and vampires don't co-exist. One is the hunter and one is the prey. Simple, right? Not for newly-turned vampire Alyssa. A surprise confrontation with Santino Vitale, the Acta Sanctorum's most fearsome hunter, sends her fleeing back to the world she once knew, and Fallon, the human friend she's missed more than anything. Now she has some explaining to do. However, that will have to wait. With the Acta Sanctorum hot on their heels, staying alive is more important than educating a human on the finer points of bloodlust.

Book 3: Pandora's Box - After a few months as a vampire, Alyssa thought she'd learned all she needed to know about the supernatural world. But her confidence is shattered by the delivery of a mysterious package - a Pandora's Box. Seemingly innocuous, the box is in reality an ancient prison, generated by a magic more powerful than anyone in her clan has ever known. But what manner of evil could need such force to contain it? When the box is opened, the sinister creature within is released, and only supernatural blood will satiate its thirst. The clan soon learns how it feels when the hunter becomes the hunted.

Book 4: Soulstone - It's a desperate time for rookie vampire Alyssa, and her sanity is hanging by a slender thread. Her clan is still reeling from the monumental battle with Aniketos; a battle that claimed the body of Lysander, her sire and lover, and trapped his spirit in a mysterious crystal. A Soulstone. Unfortunately, no amount of magic has been able to release Lysander's spirit, and the stone is starting to fade. Weeks of effort have proved futile. Her clan, the Peregrinus, have all but given up hope. Only Alyssa still believes her lover can be released. In despair, Alyssa begs the help of the local witch coven, and unwittingly exposes the supernaturals of Boston to unwanted attention from the Acta Sanctorum. The Saints converge on the city and begin their cleansing crusade to rid the world of all things "Unnatural." In the middle of an all-out war, but no closer to a solution to the dying stone, Alyssa is left with an unenviable choice: save her mate, or save her clan.

Book 5: Moonlight

Good girls don't wear fur, or fight over men, and they certainly don't run around naked, howling at the moon. But then, no-one ever called Fallon a good girl. As a human *unofficially* mated to an Alpha werewolf, Fallon is being pressured to "become"...or be gone. Her mate Aiden, the interim leader of the Olde Town Pack, is in a position that demands he either choose a wolf mate...or leave the pack forever. No matter how hot the sex with Fallon is, he can't ignore centuries of tradition. Become a wolf or not. If only the choice were that simple. Fallon's options are further clouded by the overt presence of other females desperate to be the Alpha's mate. And when these bitches get serious, it's not just claws that come out. If Fallon wants to keep her man and take the title she'll have to exert a little dominance of her own.

Book 6: Dark Salvation

A gathering storm of violence is on the horizon. Whispered threats of the Acta Sanctorum's return have the supernatural world abuzz. Only recently aware of the other world hidden behind our own, Kitara Vanders has barely scratched the surface of what being supernatural truly means. A special woman in her own right, she possesses unique telepathic abilities, gifts that have recently come under the scrutiny of the Acta Sanctorum, a fanatical organization whose mission is to cleanse the world of anything supernatural. Targeted, and marked for death, Kitara's only hope lies with the lethally seductive yet emotionally scarred warrior, Nicholas.

Knowing full well the atrocities the Acta Sanctorum is capable of, Nicholas is all too eager for the battle to begin. Fueled by pain and rage from the loss of his mate, he's itching for a fight, but one thing stands in his way, Kitara: a beautiful dark-haired woman with unique psychic abilities and an unusual link to the Saints. Despite his resolve to remain focused on his mission, a purely physical relationship binds them together in a way neither of them expected. And when her life hangs in the balance, Nicholas finds his own is teetering on the edge too.

ABOUT THE AUTHOR

Katie Salidas is a Super Woman! Endowed with special powers and abilities, beyond those of mortal women, She can get the munchkin off to gymnastics, cheerleading, Girl Scouts, and swim lessons. She can put hot food on the table for dinner while assisting with homework, baths, and bedtime... And, She still finds the time to keep the hubby happy (nudge nudge wink wink). She can do all of this and still have time to write.

And if you can believe all of those lies, there is some beautiful swamp land in Florida for sale...

Katie Salidas resides in Las Vegas, Nevada. Mother, wife, and author, she does try to do it all, often causing sleep deprivation and many nights passed out at the computer. Writing books is her passion, and she hopes that her passion will bring you hours of entertainment.

Find Katie Salidas online at:

http://www.katiesalidas.com/

Facebook
http://www.facebook.com/pages/Katie-Salidas-Author/214780936916

LinkedIn
http://www.linkedin.com/profile?viewProfile=&key=58814031&trk=tab_pro

Twitter
http://twitter.com/QuixoticKatie